THE
ECHO
OF
FOOTPRINTS

ARVIN CHAWLA

ISBN: 978-1-54397-895-7 (print)
ISBN: 978-1-54397-896-4 (ebook)

For Simar, Neety & Kamna
"Life is a thrill because I know you are in all my tomorrows"

For
dear Aneesa Aapa
+
Ilyas Bhai
With Best Wishes
AChawla

PROLOGUE

THE TEAM MOVED IN A SINGLE FILE. THE PACE WAS slow but measured. They looked like astronauts in their Personal Protection Equipment gear. The streets of Majra, a small village in northern India, were deserted. Scraps of paper swirled and played in the light breeze. Abandoned, lifeless homes lined the narrow streets on both sides. A few stray dogs, hiding in the shadows of the dilapidated structures, eyed the bizarre-looking figures, in their bright blue protective isolation suits. Sunlight glinted off the face visors. They came upon a wide area, where two streets converged. Shuttered shops stood all around. The storefront signs were dusty, but still legible—Bicycle Repair, Saree Palace, Barber Shop. An empty commuter bus straddled the middle of the road, with a huge Bollywood billboard on its side. Faces of movie stars, with their vacant Velcro smiles, stared absurdly at the desolate landscape. The four suited figures in the front of the line paused and took in the stark silence. All were reminded of the tragedy that took life away from this village in such a gruesome manner.

Arthik shut his eyes and hung his head. He looked at the figure next to him.

"I want to go to my house, Colonel," he said. His voice was muffled from behind the visor.

Colonel Biswas, of the Indian Army, looked at him with lips closed tight.

"Are you sure, Arthik?" asked Dr. John Eters, of the CDC.

Arthik nodded in the affirmative, not trusting himself to speak.

"Lead the way," Colonel Biswas said.

Arthik shuffled towards the fork in the street square. His mind drifted to a time, roughly 25 years ago....

Rain pelted down in sheets. The streets of Majra were turning into rivulets. The earthen smell of moist soil filled the small brick house. Ram Gopal Sharma looked at the freshly paved patio in the backyard and cursed. He had told the mason earlier this morning to hold off. The clouds had looked threatening then and now were letting loose. He had to cover the patio before the hail came down. He rushed to the garage and grabbed the roll of tarp. He opened the door to the patio and took a deep breath.

Five-year-old Arthik couldn't understand what his father was doing. He stood behind his father and looked around his legs at the rain outside. He had always wanted to run outside in the rain, wondering what it would feel like. He looked up and saw his father mouthing words he had not heard before. And then he saw his father run out into the rain, struggling with the roll of tarp. He stumbled a little, and his feet ploughed into the still soft patio floor. His father managed to get to the other side of the patio, leaving a trail of footprints, carved out on the freshly paved concrete.

Arthik's eyes followed his father, his mouth open. He turned around and saw his mother busy in the kitchen. He stepped through the door into the rain, with excitement and a little apprehension. His father couldn't get mad at him for playing in the rain. He himself was outside playing, wasn't he?

The pounding rain was like a thousand tiny tickle spots on his face, and Arthik squealed in delight. He stepped gingerly into the footprints left by his father and followed them to him. He got to his father and wrapped his small body around his leg. His father looked down at him and frowned. Arthik looked up at him, his eyes shut tight to avoid the hail pellets, which had started to come down. The next instant his father melted into a loud guffaw, wrapping him in his arms and swinging him high into the air.

The next morning when the mason came to repair the patio, he smoothened out the rough edges and the small pits from the hail, but he left the footprints as they were, as per instructions from Mr. Sharma.

So, there they were, tiny footprints dwarfed by larger ones, stretching from one end of the patio to the other. As the concrete dried, the markings became more distinct. Each footprint developed its own identity, its own character.

CHAPTER 1

About 1 year ago......

ARTHIK LOOKED OUT THE OVAL WINDOW OF THE 747 at the flashing red light on the wing. He strained his eyes to see through the darkness to the landscape below. A thin film of ice seemed to have formed on the outside of the window panel, making the scene pitch black. The window seat at 35,000 feet wasn't worth the 500 rupees he had slipped the check-in clerk at the New Delhi airport. Maybe he would get a good view when the plane landed at Baltimore in the early evening. His six-foot-plus frame was cramped in the seat. Next time he would request an aisle seat. At least he would be able to stretch his legs. The white gentleman next to him was sleeping. He looked comfortable under the airline's plaid blanket.

Arthik plopped the tiny pillow behind his neck and shut his eyes. The gentle snoring next to him had a soporific effect, and he began to doze off. Images flashed in his brain. The blur of lights as the plane took off from New Delhi, his family waving good-bye as he entered the airport terminal. His father, as usual, was stoic. His mother and 15-year-old sister shed a steady stream of tears. He slipped deeper into the realms of sleep, his subconscious taking him back a few years….

Arthik heard the monsoon showers smacking down on the asphalt outside the GATKA Training Academy as he changed into his regular clothes in the locker room. It was getting late. All the other students had left. His 70-year-old Gatka teacher, Mr. Zorawar Singh, was in the front wrapping up the day's work and putting away the tools of this ancient North Indian martial arts—the "lathis" or stout wooden sticks, about 6 feet in length and a couple of inches thick. There was a loud crashing sound. Arthik paused a second. It was probably thunder. He put his Gatka clothes in his shoulder bag.

"Aaaagh!" emanated from the front. This was no thunder. It sounded like Mr. Singh. Arthik rushed to the front and stared at the scene unfolding before him. Three men, with bandanas covering their faces, were pummeling the 70-year-old Mr. Singh. Blood dripped from his nose. He held his hands up, trying to protect himself.

"Where's the money, you old fuck—" one of them screamed, as he kicked him in the abdomen. Mr. Singh tumbled to the floor. As he fell, his eyes caught Arthik's. There was a strange calmness in his gaze, despite his obvious physical agony. In that split second, Arthik understood the message in his teacher's eyes. He wasn't asking for help. It was okay not to come forward. "You won't be able to handle all three of them," Mr. Singh's eyes told him. Arthik stood rooted in the shadows, his heart pounding. He was surprised he felt no fear. Only indecision— whether to jump in or not. The three thugs had not seen him yet. One of them pulled out a kukri knife and advanced towards the fallen man. Light glinted off the curved, smooth blade of the kukri.

"I'm going to cut you up into little pieces!" he screamed and raised the kukri.

Something inside Arthik snapped at that instant. He jumped forward and stood between the fallen Mr. Singh and the knife-wielding man.

"No, Arthik, no!" Mr. Singh shouted in a feeble voice. "Run...save yourself."

Arthik didn't seem to hear. His mind blocked off everything else. The three men were taken aback. There was a momentary pause.

"We don't want to hurt you. Run away, get lost," the man with the knife said, looking at Arthik.

Arthik remained silent. He bent down slowly, keeping his eyes on the man with the knife all the time, and picked up one of the Gatka sticks lying on the floor. He crouched and held his hands out, holding the stick, to attain the attack posture, as if entering a Gatka duel.

"Screw him. Cut him up too," the second man yelled. "We don't have time for this bullshit."

Arthik took two quick steps towards the man with the kukri, and before any one of them could react, he brought down the lathi on the arm holding the knife in one lightning stroke. The sound of the bone snapping was sickening, and the knife clattered onto the concrete floor.

"You broke my arm!" The injured man looked down at his mangled limb, his eyes wide open. "You broke my fuckin' arm." His voice carried a hefty dose of incredulity. "Kill the mothafucka…"

The other two men were stunned for a moment at the precise savagery of Arthik's blow. They took a couple of hesitant steps, moving towards him. One of them had a knife in his hand now. The blade was about 6 inches long, with a curved edge. The man with the broken arm staggered to his feet. He moved towards Arthik from the side and tried to kick him in the shin, letting out a string of foul curses.

Arthik's eyes were slits. He jumped straight up and, while in midair, splayed his legs, turning a full 360 degrees. His right foot caught the chin of the man with the broken arm, with his full weight behind his foot. It was the same, precise, quick savage blow resulting in the same crunching, sickening sound of the jawbone being almost pulverized. Arthik landed on his feet, still facing the speechless men. The man with the broken arm and now a broken jaw, fell to the ground and lay motionless.

"How the fuck did he do that?" gasped one of the men, taking an involuntary step backwards. The other man just swallowed hard.

Arthik crouched and held his hands out again, holding the lathi horizontally. Mr. Singh had propped himself against the wall, and a sly smile touched his bruised face.

"You know you will take them down, Arthik. The only question is how." His voice echoed in Arthik's ears.

The two men seemed to have recovered from the initial shock. Arthik knew he had to move fast, before they regrouped. He took a step towards them. The man with the knife raised his arm, and rushed towards him. Arthik took a step sideways and raised the lathi to meet the arc of the descending knife. As the knife made contact with the thick wooden lathi, Arthik knelt on his right knee and raised his arms above his head. He jerked his hands behind his head, and the man with the knife went flying over him by the force of his own momentum and crashed into the wall. He lay motionless, with his neck at an odd angle.

"Is he…is he dead?" the third man whispered, almost to himself. He couldn't take his eyes off the fallen man.

Arthik kept quiet. He was the aggressor now. Two down, one to go. The corner of his right eye locked on the 10-pound dumbbells lying against the wall, about six feet to his right. Arthik made a tumbling somersault towards the wall, and in one smooth movement dropped his lathi and picked up one of the dumbbells and threw it towards the man. The man had turned partially to follow Arthik's tumble, and the dumbbell caught him flush in the face. He fell backwards. The green bandana, still covering the lower part of his face, rapidly started to stain red.

"You are a devil!" he screamed, eyes wide with fear. He staggered up and started to back away.

Arthik picked up another dumbbell and moved towards him slowly, his eyes narrow slits.

"Let him go, Arthik," Mr. Singh said, his voice a little stronger now.

Arthik paid no heed to Mr. Singh. He had to get this guy down. He wanted to hurt him, see blood spurting, hear the crunch of bones breaking. He shifted the dumbbell to his right hand, and started to move towards the now retreating, fearful third man. His mind raced with possible permutations and movements to get him down. The man turned around and ran out the door, with Arthik in pursuit. The hunter was now the hunted. The man sloshed through puddles, with rain coming down steadily. He looked back to see Arthik gaining ground. At that moment, Arthik let go of the 10-pound dumbbell like a bowling ball. The missile caught the third man on the back of the shoulder and he fell forward, face in wet mud. Arthik caught up with him in a couple of seconds. The man on the ground looked up at Arthik and mumbled something, his eyes pleading. The steady spattering of rain on the asphalt drowned out his voice. Arthik kicked him in the ribs and grabbed the front of his shirt, standing him up like a rag doll. He spit in the man's face and started to shake him…

CHAPTER 2

ARTHIK WOKE UP TO A GENTLE JOSTLE ON HIS SHOUL-
der. It was the gentleman on the next seat, pointing to the
flight attendant.

"Please put your seat in the upright position," she said with a
smile. "We are about to land."

"Thanks," Arthik said.

He looked out of the window. He craned his neck to take
in the scenery below. Large swaths of trees and houses rapidly
grew bigger as the jumbo prepared to land. It looked so clean, so
symmetrical. The houses created long, curvy lines as if mimicking
a snake. Blacktop roads between the houses ran in different direc-
tions and sometimes ended in a cul-de-sac circle. He wondered at
the clearly designed and planned layout of the houses and roads,
a far cry from New Delhi, which was a haphazardly spread city,
enveloped in a dusty haze.

The bird's-eye view of the city below looked like a page out of an architectural book. And so many trees. Was there a forest in Baltimore? His friend had not mentioned that. He leaned back and shut his eyes for a moment and mouthed a small prayer. *God, please let me get through customs without a problem. Damn that bottle of spiced pickle.*

Months of planning and preparing were going to bear fruit today. He was finally in America. The gentle jolt of the tires on the tarmac broke Arthik's reverie. He looked out the window again, and the airport buildings whisked by in a blur. The excitement gave way to mild apprehension. Arthik felt flushed. His ears burned, and a thin film of perspiration formed on his forehead. He squirmed in his seat and took a deep breath.

"First time in the States?" a voice near him asked.

Arthik turned and looked at the man sitting next to him, as the plane taxied towards the arrival gate. A wrinkled, kind face, a mane of thick, silvery-white hair and a full smile. He had slept most of the flight and hadn't uttered a word till now.

"Yes, sir," Arthik replied, lips curving into a weak smile.

"Somebody picking you up?"

"Yes, sir. A friend."

"You'll be fine then. I'm Henry. Welcome to America." He extended his hand.

"Thank you, sir." Arthik offered his hand to a vice-like grip. *This guy will break my fingers.*

"What's your name?" Henry asked.

"Arthik Sharma."

"Artic?"

"A-r-t-h-i-k."

"I'll just call you Art. Okay?"

"It's okay, sir." Arthik's smile lost all trace of worry. He had heard of this. Indian names being Americanized. Suman became Su, Joginder became Jo, Krishan became Kris. This was exciting. He had not yet gotten off the plane, and he was already Art from Arthik. His smile widened.

"Remember a few things here, son. In this country, your handshake should be firm, your demeanor gentle, and don't call anybody 'sir' unless he's your father. Remember this, and you'll go a long way."

"Okay, sir…I mean, Henry," Arthik said, with a hint of a smile.

"There you go, Art. How come you speak such good English?" Henry asked, as the massive plane rolled to a gentle stop.

"A legacy the British left behind. Lots of schools in India have their curriculum in English," Arthik replied. The passengers were on their feet now and opening the overhead bins.

Henry got up too, and Arthik followed suit. He had to keep his head low to avoid hitting the overhead bins.

"You got a bag up here, Art?" Henry asked.

"Yes," Arthik said. "The green bag with a big label."

"Here you go," Henry said as he handed over Arthik's bag.

"Thank you." Arthik removed his light jacket and shoved it in the carry-on bag. He stretched to release the stiffness of the long flight out of his muscles.

"You a body-builder or something?" Henry asked, as he watched Arthik's muscles ripple as he stretched.

"Oh, no. Not anymore," Arthik smiled. "Just work out regularly." He pulled out his new cashmere *Monte Carlo* sweater and slipped it on.

There was about a five-minute wait before the doors opened, and then everybody shuffled towards the exit.

"Thank God. Need to get out and stretch my legs," Henry murmured.

Arthik managed a weak smile. The anxiety and apprehension were returning. The air-conditioning was off now. A smatter of conversation rose among tired faces.

What about that bottle of spiced pickle? He looked at the disembarkation form he had filled out before landing.

"Food, vegetables not allowed," he read again.

Sweat ran down his neck. *Could they arrest me?*

Calm down, Arthik, you are being stupid. It's not poison, for God's sake.

He took a deep breath as the line started to move slowly. Why did Avtar have to insist on that damn pickle. Arthik couldn't say no to him. Avtar was the friend picking him up today. And not only that—Arthik was going to stay with Avtar until he found his own apartment. How could he say no to the person who was sponsoring him?

Arthik followed the rest of the passengers to the ramp that led to the terminal. Everything was so clean. Bright neon lights and shiny tile floors gleamed. "Baggage Claim" pointed down the stairs. Arthik braced himself for the rush and jostling as all the passengers headed towards the narrow passage leading to the stairs. The pushing and shoving never came. The crowd slowed, voices hushed polite apologies, some people chose to yield the way to the other passengers. *This is different from India, all so orderly.* A flight of stairs led to a big hall with baggage claim. A big belt rolled around with a few bags, making squeaking noises. Arthik went up to the revolving belt to examine the bags being revealed through the plastic-curtained chute. He kept fidgeting and wiped sweat off his brow. He looked around for a cart but didn't see any.

"Hey Art…" a voice boomed, making him jump.

"Oh, hello, Henry," Arthik smiled at the familiar face. His eyes strayed to the cart Henry was pushing.

"You need a cart?"

"Yes, I have two bags."

"Go around that corner, and you'll find a whole bunch of them." Henry pointed towards the other side of the belt.

Arthik nodded and picked up his carry-on bag.

"You can leave your bag here. I'll watch it," Henry said.

Arthik hesitated for a second. His face burned. *Can I leave the bag here with an almost total stranger? But it would be so impolite to say no.* Multiple scenarios rushed through his brain.

He looks honest.

"Okay…I'll be right back," Arthik mumbled. He took quick steps towards the short line for carts.

He couldn't see his bag or Henry from the cart carousel. After a couple of minutes, he was at the head of the line. Arthik realized that he had to insert money in the slot to free a cart from the stand. He squinted at the dollar amount.

"*Three* dollars?" he mumbled to himself. *That's 180 rupees.* For a brief second, he wondered if he could haul the bags himself, but then discarded the thought. Everything he owned in the world was packed into those two suitcases. He got three crisp dollar bills from his wallet and put them in the slot.

He hurried back to Henry with his newly rented baggage cart. *Oh, God, hope he's not run away with my carry-on.* A spontaneous smile lit up his face when he saw Henry standing guard over his bag.

I shouldn't be so suspicious. Americans are honest.

"The bags are coming through now. Good luck, Art."

"Thank you, sir," Arthik said.

"Hey—I told you not to 'sir' me. Let's see that grip again," Henry smiled and offered his hand.

"It was very nice to meet you, Henry." Arthik took the large man's hand in a firm grip.

"You're learning already," Henry said and walked towards the belt to retrieve his bags.

Arthik pushed his cart towards the baggage belt and spotted one of his bags. Images of the polythene-wrapped pickle bottle hidden inside the bag flashed in his thoughts. Would the aroma of the spiced pickle permeate through the multiple plastic layers? His heart raced as he collected his bags. He took a deep breath through his nose.

I think I can smell it.

The cart suddenly felt heavy as he pushed it towards the "Non-Citizens" line. His heart did a somersault when he saw a uniformed custom agent with a big dog on a leash coming towards their line. The dog randomly sniffed bags in front of the line. He froze as the dog passed by.

Damn the pickle.

A couple ahead of him conversed in native Punjabi. Out of the corner of his eye, he saw a uniformed guard walk out of the hall with the dog. He wiped his brow and moved forward with the line.

After a few minutes, it was Arthik's turn at the counter.

"Sharma, Artik?" asked the pleasant-looking middle-aged woman, peering from behind her big glasses.

"Yes, ma'am. ArT-H-ik Sharma."

"Hi, welcome to the United States," she smiled. "Can I please see your passport and papers?"

Arthik handed over the papers.

"Your date of birth is February 8th, 1987… and you are here on an immigrant visa?"

Arthik nodded. She flipped through the passport and stamped it.

"You are all set, Mr. Sharma. Please follow the green line to the customs station."

"Thank you." Arthik pushed his cart ahead, as his eyes followed the green line on the floor. He swallowed when he saw more uniformed agents on the other side of the huge hall-like room, checking bags.

Damn…damn the pickle…

Could he take it out now and throw it in the trash? His eyes darted, frantically looking for a trashcan. There was none. There were too many people around anyway. He probably would be jumped by security if he took out a polythene-wrapped one-liter bottle out of his bag. His legs felt like lead as he pushed his cart towards the "U. S. Customs" sign. The banging inside his chest grew louder. A trickle of sweat traced down the side of his face as he approached a tall uniformed customs agent. His cashmere sweater seemed to develop a thousand tiny needles that jabbed him.

"This way, sir," the agent said in a surprisingly soft voice, pointing to the lane in front of his desk.

Arthik maneuvered his cart towards him.

I'm going to end up in jail....

"You got any food, live plants, seeds, grains…." The agent rattled off a practiced list.

"No, sir…, nothing," Arthik managed to get out and handed him the customs declaration form that he had filled out in the plane.

The tall agent glanced at the bags and took a measured look at Arthik, then waved him on.

"Is that all? Am I done?" Arthik stood rooted to the spot.

"Yep. All done." The uniformed agent turned his attention to the next person in line.

Arthik's posture straightened, and he pushed his cart with renewed energy. The neon lights shone brighter, the tiled floor gleamed, and people seemed happier.

The spiced pickle had not been a problem.

CHAPTER 3

ARTHIK SMILED BACK AT AN ELDERLY COUPLE AS HE made his way to the passenger pick-up ramp. He adjusted his watch to the current time. Avtar had said he would be at the airport after work at about 6 p.m. It was 3:30 p.m. He had some time to browse around the airport. He turned his attention to the brightly lit signs that were strung along the sides of the wide airport lobby. People scurried along, some pushing strollers, others pushing carts. Some stood in front of the big electronic screens, looking for their flights. He took all this in, fascinated by the abundance of color and vibrancy.

This place is huge, he thought to himself.

All the hustle and bustle seemed to have a purpose. There was nobody just lounging around, but there was something else. The airport seemed happy. Busy, but happy. And the colors—so many and so bright—clothes, walls, motifs, and even the people.

I'm going to make this move to the USA work. I must, for my family.

He walked across to the "All News" store. A young couple stood at the entrance in a tight embrace. As Arthik went by them, they locked their lips and the embrace became tighter. Arthik stared. A voice in the back of his mind told him it was not polite or appropriate to stare, but his eyes were glued on the couple. Then their hands started moving, and Arthik's mouth fell open as his face reddened. He had heard about Americans not being shy to show their affection, but wasn't this too much? He managed to pry his eyes away and looked at other people around them. Nobody even glanced at the couple. A scene like this would cause a riot back home.

The fragrance of fried potatoes wafted, and Arthik's stomach growled. He followed his nose and found himself in front of a McDonald's. He stood in line and waited his turn.

"Would you like to try one of our combos today?"

Arthik looked up at the distinct Indian accent. The lapel badge said "Sanjay."

"I just came from India." Arthik smiled.

"Welcome, ji." Sanjay smiled back. "What would you like?"

"Grilled chicken combo. I'm here on a permanent visa."

"Wonderful. For here or to go?" Sanjay threw french fries on the grill.

"Beg your pardon? I don't want anything else," Arthik said.

"I meant are you going to eat here, or are you going to take it home?" Sanjay smiled.

"Oh…" Arthik was red faced. "I'm sorry, I am going to eat here."

"Don't worry, ji. It took me six months to get the hang of 'for here or to go.' Where are you from in India?"

"From Majra. It's a small town next to Chandigarh."

"Ah. I have a friend from Chandigarh. Here you are." Sanjay handed him the food. "Good luck."

"Thank you." Arthik got his food and pushed his cart close to the chairs.

The grilled chicken sandwich was good and the fries bland. There was no masala flavor, like they added back home. Or was this home now? It didn't feel right, calling this home. Too soon.

I haven't stepped outside the airport yet, for God's sake.

But he couldn't go back. No way. Not after the way he left India. He just had to make this work, had to be successful. And soon. This was going to be his home, no matter what. His family was depending on him. Images of his kid sister flashed…

"Who will help me with my homework?" Meenu had mumbled between tears.

"You have friends. And these five years will go by so fast—"

"Five years? I'm fourteen now…you won't recognize me," she said between sobs.

"Arre pagli, you all will be with me in five years. In between, I'll be making trips here almost every year. Stop crying. I need you to be strong for me." Arthik took her in his arms and his stomach clenched. A little unease slipped in then—was he doing the right thing?

His father had walked in at that time and took in the situation in an instant—like he always did.

"Hey, kiddos, dinner's ready. And then let's get some shopping done for Arthik. He can't go to America with just pajamas." He gently pulled Meenu towards him and held her. "Your mother and I will be here with you, every second. So why do you worry?"

Meenu smiled and nodded as she walked out of the room. Arthik mouthed a "thank you" to his dad.

"You stay strong, son. From the inside, in your heart. We'll look after her. All of us will be fine," he said.

Arthik knew she would be. Over the years he had come to realize that his father was special. He didn't say much, but he meant every word. He looked at his father.

"Am I doing the right thing? Leaving you all to go to America?"

His father paused for a moment. "Any father who tells his child that he is happy to see him go is lying. But it would be selfish of me to insist that you stay. I am happy for you. You have to chart your own destiny. Come with me."

Arthik followed his father to the rear patio.

"Do you see those footprints? You remember how they came about?" His father pointed to the imprints from decades ago.

Arthik looked down at the patio. Tiny footprints dwarfed by large ones. He had seen these cursorily many times over the years. He got down on his knees and brushed away the leaves and dust around one of them. *The impression became clearer, and he stared at it for a long moment. The footprints had meaning today.*

"I see them, father," Arthik said. "And I remember." And he did, the stormy day more than two decades ago.

"The small footprint is within the big one, but it still has its own identity. You will always be a part of me, wherever you are. We are bound together by blood."

"Yes, father."

"Whenever I miss you, I'll come here and look at these footprints." His father paused. "Look at you. From a body builder to Gatka champion. And now to America."

Arthik stood up. "Yeah. You never know what's coming next."

"Your Gatka teacher, Mr. Singh, still calls. He's convinced you could have restored Gatka to its original glory."

Arthik smiled. "I guess that was not my destiny. Not my calling. Not after that day at the academy." Arthik shuddered as he recalled that fateful day three years ago.

"You still blame yourself for that incident? They were trying to steal, those scum. It was lucky your class ran late that day at the academy."

"But I almost killed them, father. With my bare hands. I realized that day I have this terrible skill. The curse of this uncontrolled rage."

"All three of them were okay. Nobody died," his father said.

"Yeah. After two months in the hospital," Arthik said, shaking his head. "Anyway, like you said—that's not your destiny. Now go get Dada. He'll be in his room or with his chickens in the backyard. Let's eat."

"Yes, father." Arthik hugged his father and held him tight for a long couple of seconds. His eyes moistened, but he was careful not to let his father see.

Arthik walked to the backyard to look for his grandfather. All he saw was a few hens running around. His grandfather spent most of his day feeding and petting them. He walked over to his grandfather's room. And there he was, as always. Sitting ramrod straight on his chair, watching the news channel. He looked a lot younger than his 97 years. A mane of silver hair and a flowing white beard defined his appearance, but his mind had slipped in the last few years. A few hens sat around his chair. In all, there were about 20 hens, all pearly white, who followed his grandfather all day. There was an ancient village folklore—that having white hens around was a good omen. And having hens that were of any other color was not considered auspicious. So in Majra, there were only white hens.

"Dada ji, let's eat," Arthik said, as he put his arm around his grandfather's shoulders.

"Who is it? Arthik?" Dada peered from behind his bushy eyebrows.

"Yes, Dada. It's Arthik. Let's eat." Arthik helped him up.

Dada walked a few steps and stopped. "You are going to America?" he asked, looking at Arthik.

"Yes, Dada, I am," Arthik said, feeling emptiness in the pit of his stomach.

"I'll miss you," Dada said and walked on slowly to the dining room.

Arthik stood there, awash with guilt. He caught up to his grandfather and gave him a bear hug. "I'll miss you too, Dada." He was surprised at the strength of his grandfather's hug.

"But you should go, Arthik. Follow your dreams. Be honest and sincere in your work and success will kiss your feet."

"I will, Dada. I will." Arthik helped his grandfather onto a chair at the dining table.

CHAPTER 4

BACK AT THE BWI AIRPORT, ARTHIK ADJUSTED HIS
watch to Eastern Standard Time. An hour left. He remembered
Avtar's instructions—walk up the passenger pick-up ramp and
wait by the curb.

"And look for a Burgundy Toyota Camry—V6."

He had detected pride in Avtar's voice over the phone. And
why not? Avtar had been in America for just three years, and
he was already driving a Camry! Arthik didn't know what V6
meant—probably a luxury model or something. He walked up
the ramp and stepped outside. The first thing that struck him was
the absence of honking. He stood still for a second. Cars whizzed
by, some tourist buses, and an occasional patrol car. But the only
sound was the muted roar of engines and rubber pounding the
asphalt. Unlike New Delhi, where you generally had to shout
above the cacophony of multiple honks to make conversation.
It seemed unreal, the traffic flowing by and not a single honk.

This was going to take time getting used to. He settled down on a wooden bench by the curbside.

"Hey, Arthik," a voice yelled from a Toyota Camry that had pulled up beside him.

"Avtar! *Arre yaar*, I didn't see your car," Arthik said, as he got up.

"You're looking good," Avtar said as he embraced him in a generous hug. "Let's get your stuff in the car."

"Thank you, you look good yourself." Arthik was not being entirely truthful. Avtar seemed to have gained weight at the wrong places since he had seen him last. His moderate-sized paunch pushed through his loose T-shirt.

"Good…good. Great to see you," Avtar said. "How are your folks doing?"

"All doing well, Avtar. How's life treating you here?"

"Oh, I'm hanging in here. It's a busy life, but it goes on," he replied.

On the way to Avtar's apartment, Arthik looked at the maze of ramps and criss-crossing flyovers.

"How do you know which way to go?" Arthik asked, with widened eyes.

"It's very simple, Arthik. You'll be zipping on these roads in a few weeks. So have things changed much at home?"

"Not much. I got the pickle for you."

"You managed it? Was it any trouble?" Avtar asked.

"Oh, no. Not at all," Arthik replied, without missing a beat.

"How's your kid sister…Meenu, isn't it?"

"She'll be fine." Arthik took a deep breath. "She was a little upset."

Avtar nodded and concentrated on driving. It had started to drizzle, and light scattered on the windshield.

"This is your bedroom, Arthik," Avtar said, pointing towards a closed door. "The bathroom is in the hallway and that's the kitchen. It's not much, but works for a single guy."

"Thank you," Arthik said. "I hope I can find a job soon and then I can rent my own apartment."

"No rush, man. You relax for a few days. I've a friend who works at the 7-Eleven nearby. He promised to help."

Avtar went into the kitchen and came back with a bottle of Johnnie Walker Black Label scotch whiskey and a couple of glasses. "Soda or water?" he asked.

"No. I don't drink."

"Are you serious? C'mon, man, have a drink. It's Black Label. You'll sleep well," Avtar said.

"Okay, Avtar," Arthik said, wringing his hands.

Ice clinked in the glasses, and Avtar poured the whiskey.

"It doesn't taste bad," Arthik said, staring at the amber drink in his glass.

"Bad? Sweetest taste in the world, man. The sweetest." Avtar downed his drink in one big gulp.

"Wow," Arthik said, his brow arched. "That was impressive."

"You ain't seen nothing yet," Avtar said as he poured himself another stiff drink. "So how are things back home, really?"

"Same old stuff. The rich are getting richer, and poor are getting poorer. It's a vicious cycle."

"And how about you—still get tongue-tied around the ladies?" Avtar let out a chuckle. He looked at Arthik's torso where a well-built body was barely hidden under the old, threadbare T-shirt.

Arthik bristled. "No. I'm better now." He swirled the ice in his glass.

"With a body like yours, ladies will line up for you. In America, you've got to exude confidence. Whether you feel it inside or not." Avtar carried on. "And if you want to score with the ladies, you got to be smooth."

"Uh-huh," Arthik mumbled.

In the next 30 minutes, with half the bottle gone, Arthik was still on his first drink.

"C'mon, you got to have another one," Avtar said. His eyes were bloodshot now.

"No, thanks," Arthik said. "I think I'm ready to go to bed." He stood up, and suddenly the whole world wobbled. He grabbed the table for support.

"Whoa!" he exclaimed sheepishly.

"Man, you're shaky after one drink?" Avtar frowned. "Is this the first time you are drinking whiskey?"

Arthik nodded sheepishly. "First time, any kind of alcohol."

"Wow. I'll get you on track," Avtar said. "You want to eat something?"

"No, thanks. I ate at the airport. You got to work tomorrow?"

"Yeah. Leave at seven a.m. I loaded the refrigerator for you. You'll be able to fix something for yourself?"

"Oh, yes, don't worry about me. I'll manage. I'll take a walk around the neighborhood tomorrow," Arthik said.

"You do that. And call India in the morning. Talk to your folks. I know they'll be waiting for your call."

"I will," Arthik replied. "I'll make it quick. I know it's expensive to call overseas from here."

"It's really not expensive at all. I have a good plan. Don't worry about the cost," Avtar said. "You talk as long as you want to. And tomorrow when you go out, don't go too far. This area can be dicey sometimes."

"Dicey? What do you mean?" Arthik asked.

"Just stay within half a mile of the apartment. We'll start working on your driver's license in a couple of days. I'll be back at six in the evening. Good night," Avtar said.

"Good night." Arthik walked carefully to his room and started to unpack. He carried the bottle of spiced pickle to the kitchen. He was glad he smuggled it in…it was the least he could do for Avtar. He lay down and shut his eyes. Muddled images flashed.

Five-year-old Arthik running in his backyard amidst the monsoon rain, stepping into his father's footprints on the freshly laid patio. Then his father emerged in his subconscious, and he didn't look happy. He seemed to be frowning at the Black Label Johnnie Walker. The jumbled freeways….the enthusiastic couple in a passionate lip-lock…Zorawar Singh, his Gatka teacher, in the background. "Move faster, kick harder." His voice was an echo. "In the world we live in, you never know when you might have to defend yourself." His voice faded.

Then Arthik's brain gave in to the soothing blankness. He tossed and turned all night. The fatigue of the long journey and the culmination of his desire to come to America kept his subconscious in a semi-animated state during the entirety of his first night in his new world.

CHAPTER 5

THE SILENCE WOKE UP ARTHIK. HE LAY STILL FOR A
few seconds and strained his ears. Still nothing. Nothing, but the
hum of the furnace. No screeching of scooter rickshaws, no heavy
rumble of school buses, no constant honking, *akashvani* on All
India Radio. *I can't believe I miss all that.*

He sat up, and the next instant held his head in his hands. It
felt like lead. *That whiskey!* He staggered to the bathroom. After
battling with the faucet for a bit, he splashed cold water on his
face. He then went into the kitchen and fixed himself a light breakfast. His eyes wandered to the empty bottle of whiskey on the
small dining table. There had been a quarter bottle left last night
when he went to bed. Avtar? He *finished* it?

Arthik looked at the empty bottle again and his stomach
clenched. Maybe it was an isolated binge. He took a deep breath,
and his jaw hardened. He was going to do better. He just *had* to.
Got to get a job.

Morning exercises first. He had a regimen of strenuous work-outs that he went through every morning. He then went through a series of complicated contortions and flips that would have done a gymnast proud. He was done in half an hour. He took off his sweat-drenched undershirt and lay down on the couch, gulping deep breaths. He looked at his watch. It was 10 a.m. Perfect time to call India. He picked up the phone.

"Hello?" A voice crackled from the other side. "Arthik?"

"Yes, father. I reached here safe. Are you all okay?"

"Yes, son. We are all fine. Did Avtar come to pick you up?"

"Yes, he did. He's looking after me very well. How are Ma, Dada, and Meenu?"

"They are fine, son. They miss you, of course."

"Let me talk to them."

There was a short pause.

"Hello, beta Arthik. Are you all right?"

"Yes, Ma. I'm fine. Don't worry about me. Look after yourself."

"You eat properly. Who's going to cook for you?"

"It's easy to cook here, Ma." Arthik smiled. *Typical Ma.* "Where's Meenu?"

"She's gone to her friend's house. She misses you already."

"Tell her I miss her too. I'll call you again in a couple of days, Ma. *Namaste* to Dada," Arthik said.

"Namaste, beta. God bless you."

Arthik clicked the line dead and slowly placed the phone in the charger. He felt an emptiness, and a little guilt. He sat on the couch and stared at his hands for a few long seconds. *Have I made the right decision?* He took a deep breath and got up to get ready.

Arthik walked to the strip mall near the apartment. Everything was so clean, so organized. He was struck again by the absence of honking, and the orderly traffic. And where were the people? The sidewalks were almost bare. It was very different from India, where the sidewalks and walking paths were almost choked with an exploding population.

He walked to the grocery store. It was huge, and aptly named Giant. He spotted a tall man, with distinctly South Asian features, stocking the shelves. He was probably in his mid-sixties, had a slight paunch that complemented a kind face. He looked of Indian descent. After a little hesitation, he walked up to him.

"Hello, Namaste," Arthik said, extending the traditional Indian greeting. "How are you?"

The man turned and looked at him. He was almost as tall as him. A grey beard, big spectacles with a silver rim and a kind face peered back at him. He had green overalls on, with the store logo. A silver mane of hair swept straight back onto his neck.

"I'm fine, how are you?" The voice was deep, soft, and soothing. It matched his appearance. Few people had that perfect match of voice and personality. Here was one.

"My name is Arthik Sharma. I arrived from India yesterday." He held out his hand.

"Nice to meet you, Arthik." The grip was firm. "My name is Ajeet. You here on a tourist visa?"

"No, I have a green card. I'm looking for a job. You know of any openings in this store?"

"Not at this time. So where are you staying?"

"With a friend of mine, just round the corner—Springhill Lake apartments. Till I get my own apartment," Arthik said.

Ajeet nodded. He looked at his watch. "It's break time for me. You want to come to the café with me?"

"Sure," Arthik said.

The café was a small area in one corner of the store. Again, Arthik was awed by the cleanliness, the precision of the layout, the crisp uniform of the girl behind the counter. There were donuts, cakes, salads, and sandwiches on display. Arthik peered closely and saw the price of the chicken sandwich. $3.50? Was that right? He did quick mental math and converted the price into Indian rupees. Two hundred and fifty rupees for a small sandwich?

"I thought food was cheap in America."

"It is," Ajeet replied, and looked closely at the sandwich Arthik was looking at.

"Almost two hundred and fifty rupees for a small chicken sandwich?"

Ajeet smiled. "It's cheap if you make the sandwich at home. The $3.50 also includes the price of putting it together and convenience of getting it at your work place. So what would you like to have?"

"Oh, no, thank you. I ate before I came."

"You sure?" Ajeet asked.

"Yes, thank you."

"So where are you from, Arthik?" Ajeet asked, pulling up a chair. "C'mon, have a seat."

"Majra, small town next to—"

"Chandigarh," Ajeet finished for him. "I know Punjab. I'm from Ludhiana."

Arthik felt an instant connection. He had just met Ajeet, but he felt comfortable with him as though he were an uncle not seen in years.

"How long have you been away from home?" Arthik asked.

"Forty-two years. This is home for me and my family now."

"Wow. Forty-two years. That's a long time."

"What kind of a job are you looking for?"

"Anything. Hourly work, construction, cashier. Anything. I don't have a college degree. I'm ready to do any kind of work, to get started," Arthik said.

"You are in a rush, aren't you?" Ajeet said, a faint smile crinkling the corner of his mouth.

"I have to get my parents and sister here. They are back home." Arthik stared at his hands.

Ajeet looked at the young man for a moment, searching his face. It seemed he was looking at the face of a much younger version of himself.

"You'll be fine, Arthik. You work hard, and you can get your family here in a few years."

"I mean, look at you." Arthik frowned and shook his head.

Ajeet paused and then let out a loud laugh. "You are worried you'll end up like me?"

"Well, you've been here for forty years, right?"

"Ha-ha-ha…" Ajeet could barely control himself. "I am retired. I work here to keep myself busy. I don't need to work. So, don't worry." He let out another chuckle.

"I'm…I'm sorry." Arthik's face reddened. "I shouldn't have said that."

"I like you, Arthik. I know the manager of the 7-Eleven in this plaza. He's always looking for help in his store. You come back tomorrow about five p.m. and I'll take you to him."

"Really? Thank you," Arthik said. "I hope it's no trouble. You hardly know me—"

"I might not know you, but I know people like you. You remind me of me, years ago, when I first came to America."

"I'll see you tomorrow, around five. I think my friend also mentioned something about a 7-Eleven…maybe it's the same guy," Arthik said.

"Maybe. We'll find out tomorrow."

Later that evening, Arthik relayed this conversation to Avtar.

"So, he's going to get you a job after meeting you for five minutes?" Avtar's eyebrows were arched. "And he's Indian?"

"Yeah. He seems to be a nice guy," Arthik said. "And thank you for the nice dinner, Avtar."

"You're welcome. You know, there are very few Indians who will help you selflessly. Most of them will pull you down." Avtar put the plates in the dishwasher.

"Maybe you had a few bad experiences. This guy was nice. You are helping me, aren't you?"

"Well, if it's the 7-Eleven in this plaza, the guy I know is Keith. Big, African-American guy. Wonderful person, always happy."

"I'll look for Keith," Arthik said.

"That's great. Let's celebrate," Avtar said and went into the kitchen. In a moment, he was back with a new bottle of Johnnie Walker whiskey.

"No thank you, Avtar. I had such a headache in the morning."

"Come on, man. I get a headache when I don't drink. Let's have a couple." Avtar opened the bottle.

"Okay, make me a very light one. You drink every day?" Arthik asked.

"No, only on special occasions."

And it was the same thing as the night before. Avtar gulped down drinks, and Arthik barely finished one. Half the bottle was gone in about an hour.

The next day, Arthik made his way to the same Giant grocery store. He looked at his watch. He had been eager and impatient; it was just 4:30 p.m. Still half an hour to go. His eyes paused at his own reflection on one of the glass windows. He hoped he had on the right combination of clothes to impress the manager at the 7-Eleven. Midnight blue slacks, black leather shoes, a light blue T-shirt. Serious, responsible, and ready to work. He rubbed his hands together and looked at his watch again. He made his way to the front of the Giant store.

"You couldn't wait, could you?" Ajeet's voice boomed.

Arthik turned around. "I had nothing to do at home," he said. "I'm a little early."

"That's all right," Ajeet said. "Let's go."

"Are they going to interview me?" Arthik scrambled to keep up, as they made their way to the 7-Eleven.

"They might."

A short pause followed.

"Well?" Arthik asked.

"Well what?"

"What are they going to ask me? Am I dressed right?"

Ajeet looked at him and smiled. "Don't worry. Just be yourself. That's the store straight ahead." He pointed to the store ahead. A brick outline with the typical 7-Eleven logo on top, with large, plate-glass, storefront windows. "It has a gas station and a car wash. And to the right, there's some fast food places, just in case."

Arthik's heart thumped as they entered the 7-Eleven. He wiped his hands on his slacks. His mouth was suddenly dry. He looked around the store, trying to take in all the merchandise and layout.

"Hi, Keith," Ajeet called out to the man standing behind the cash machine.

"Hey, man," Keith said. "How are you, Ajeet?"

"All good, my man. How's life treating you?" Ajeet walked up to the counter and held out his hand.

"All good, all good. Who is this strapping young man?"

"This is Arthik. He's looking for work. You still have an opening here?"

"We sure do," he said as he extended a hand out to Arthik. "Hi, I'm Keith."

"Hello, sir. My name is Arthik Sharma."

"Firm handshake. I like that. Glad to meet you, Arthik. And don't 'sir' me. Keith will do just fine," he said.

"Nice to meet you, Keith. You can call me Art," Arthik said.

Sounded strange, calling himself Art. He noticed that Ajeet cocked an eyebrow at his new nickname.

"So, when can you start working?" Keith asked.

"Whenever you want me to. I have my green card and social security number with me right now."

"Good. I'll make copies," Keith replied. "I can offer you $14 per hour. Does that sound good to you?"

"Oh, sure," Arthik said, taken aback at the quick offer.

"Can you come tomorrow at ten in the morning?"

"Sure, I can." Arthik couldn't hide the eagerness in his voice.

"I think my friend knows you—Avtar."

"Oh, yeah. Avtar. Haven't seen him in a while," Keith said. "You know, I offered him a job here."

"You did?"

"Yeah. Tell him I said hello. Anyway, we'll see you at ten in the morning. Marge will show you the ropes, and you can sign the paperwork then."

"Marge?" Arthik asked. He suddenly had butterflies in his stomach. *Marge is a girl's name.*

"She's the day-time shift manager," Keith replied. "Nice gal. She'll give you the go-around of how the place runs."

"Okay." *I have to get used to talking to girls*, Arthik told himself. He wiped his brow.

"You okay, Arthik?" Ajeet asked.

"Yeah, I'm fine."

"Well, then, I have to leave now. Thank you for helping, Keith," Ajeet said and held out his hand.

"No, thank *you*. I've been looking for a reliable person for a while."

"I'll try to do my best, sir," Arthik said.

"You can start by not calling me 'sir,'" Keith said.

"Yes, sir…I mean, Keith," Arthik smiled. "I'll be here at ten tomorrow morning."

Outside, Ajeet turned to Arthik. "You scared or something? Nervous?"

"No…no," Arthik flushed. "I'm okay."

"You don't look okay to me," Ajeet said. "Spill it."

"It's nothing. I…I just feel nervous around women," Arthik blurted, wiping his brow.

Ajeet stopped and looked at him. "Are you serious? You got to be kidding me!"

"I shouldn't have said anything. Now I'm embarrassed." A weak smile touched Arthik's face.

"I'm sorry. I didn't mean to embarrass you," Ajeet said. They walked for a few yards before he stopped. "You know, in this country, there's no difference between men and women at the workplace. So, the sooner you get used to working with women, the better off you will be."

"I'll be fine," Arthik said, shaking his head.

CHAPTER 6

THE NEXT MORNING FOUND ARTHIK IN FRONT OF THE 7-Eleven at 9:45 a.m. He had been up at 6 a.m. He ironed his blue slacks till the crease was sharp as a knife and picked out a light blue, full-sleeved shirt. He remembered to put on deodorant and hair gel, just like Avtar had told him. He also trashed the bottle of coconut hair oil that Avtar had threatened to throw away. He had been ready at 7 a.m.

Arthik walked to the empty telephone booth to the left of the store and stood beside it. He tried to peer in through the tinted glass windows, but couldn't see much. It was a beautiful day, in the middle of March. The skies were clear blue, and trees showed off their fresh foliage. But all that went unnoticed by Arthik. He couldn't keep his hands still as he waited outside and saw people going in and out of the store. He glanced at his watch again. 9:55 a.m. Time to go in.

"I'll be alright. I'll be all right," he repeated to himself as he walked towards the front door, wiping the perspiration from his hands onto his slacks.

It was much cooler inside. He waited a few seconds by the doorway to let his eyes adjust.

"Hi, you must be Art." A pleasant voice beside him made him jump.

Arthik turned around and froze for a second. He saw a petite woman, probably in her mid-twenties, with a friendly smile. Her eyes were a warm blue, white pearly teeth gleamed, and she had slightly raised cheekbones. She wore black jeans and a dark green T-shirt, with a Convenience-Café logo on the left breast pocket. She brushed aside wisps of blond hair from her face, looking up at his six-foot-plus frame.

"I'm Marge," she continued and held out her hand.

Arthik shook her hand, as his heart bounded. *She looks like an angel.*

"Hello, madam. Very pleased to meet you," he said. It took him a couple of seconds to find his voice.

"*Madam?!* You are so cute." She chuckled. "I'm Marge to my friends. C'mon back and let's get started."

Arthik followed her to a room behind the cash counter. She walked fast, but without being hurried. He couldn't help but notice her hour-glass figure. The room was small, about 10 feet by 15 feet, with one exit door at the rear. There was a small desk on one side of the room, with a rusty table lamp spilling anemic light. The three-blade ceiling fan moved lazily, announcing each completed revolution with a soft, grating *ting*.

Marge plopped on the chair behind the table. "Grab a chair, Art."

Arthik sat on one of the two chairs, facing Marge. "Thank you, madam," he said.

"Hey, Art, let's get one thing straight. You call me Marge, and you work with me and not for me. You getting me?" Marge smiled as she tried to put on a stiffer tone.

"Yes…, Marge," Arthik said, his hands fidgeting with a paper clip on the table.

"And you can also smile. You'll be fine here. Keith is a great boss and is the de facto owner. I've never seen the real owner. I'll train you on the cash register today. We'll do store stocking and inventory the next few days."

Arthik nodded. He listened to Marge intently, following every word. The nervousness was abating, eagerness to start working taking its place.

"Your shift will start at 7 a.m. and end at 5 p.m. You can grab lunch in between, around noon time. We will take turns for the lunch break. You can buy stuff from our store itself, and there are some fast food joints around the corner."

Marge got up and pointed to the TV screen on the wall in the far corner of the room.

"That's our monitor for the security cameras. We have four cameras," she said. She clicked on the remote and the screen came on, split into four equal black and white parts. "Two cameras are outside, front and back. The other two are inside. This monitor is generally on all the time, and all the activity from these cameras is recorded on a hard drive. You with me so far?"

"Yes, madam, I mean, Marge," Arthik replied, correcting himself. He stood at a respectful body length distance from her, his hands behind his back.

"Relax, Art. You look nervous." Marge stepped towards him and punched him playfully on his arm.

"No...no. I'm not nervous," Arthik mumbled, taking a step back.

"Good. Let's go to the front now and let me take you around the store."

Arthik followed her. *She's nice*, he thought to himself. *She's talking to me like a friend.* He caught up with her with an extra-long step and walked beside her. She looked up at him and smiled.

There were a few customers for the next couple of hours, and Marge went over the nuts and bolts of running the store with him. He grew more confident as the day wore on.

"Keith said he'll drop off your shirts this evening," Marge said. "You can handle the cash register now?"

Arthik nodded in the affirmative.

"Well, go behind the counter and let's get a few transactions under your belt."

Arthik went over to the cash register and put his hands on the counter. He felt good. He ran his hands over the counter, feeling the cracks and pits in the granite. The Lotto machine was placed on the left, the cigarettes were stacked on the back wall. *I am going to own a store like this one day.* Anticipation and excitement surged through him. His hands traveled the undersurface of the counter. He felt a round knob and bent down to look. He straightened up and caught Marge's eye on the other side of the store.

"What's this red button under the counter?" he asked.

"I can't believe I missed that. That's the emergency call button. Punching that would have the cops here in a few minutes."

Arthik's hand moved away quickly from the switch.

One year later…

"Hey, Arthik, I barely see you these days," Ajeet said. "What are you doing here today?"

"I'm sorry. I've been so busy," Arthik replied. "I am here to pick up some stuff for my apartment. Thanks for helping me move." There was pride in his tone.

"That was my pleasure, Arthik. You settling in good?"

"Yeah. I love it," Arthik beamed.

"And how's the job working out?" Ajeet asked.

"Good, really good. Time is just flying by. I have more responsibility in the store now," Arthik said.

"I know. Keith likes you, says you are a hard worker," Ajeet smiled. "I heard that girl likes you too."

"Girl? Which girl?" Arthik's face reddened.

"How many girls work with you at the store?" Ajeet asked.

"You mean Marge. Where did you hear that?" Arthik was blushing, without trying to hide it.

"Doesn't matter. She's a nice girl, Arthik," Ajeet said. "Take her out or something."

"I got to go now, Ajeet. I'll talk to you later." Arthik turned around and half-ran, half-walked to the checkout lane.

Ajeet smiled as he watched the retreating Arthik, and went back to work.

Arthik's heart raced as he headed to his apartment. He liked Marge a lot. Did she like him too? She must have said something for Ajeet to make a comment like that. And what did he mean, "Take her out?" Did he mean on a date? His heart pounded even more.

"I'll talk to Avtar," Arthik murmured to himself.

Arthik looked at the ominous clouds as he walked back to his apartment. He felt good, having his own apartment. He had moved into it about a month ago. He looked at his watch. It was 8:30 p.m. He waved to a couple of neighborhood kids as he went up the stairs to his studio apartment. Arthik took a deep breath and took in the fresh-paint smell, still lingering in his apartment after a month. He fixed a quick dinner. After eating, he picked up the phone and called India.

"Namaste, father. It's Arthik."

"Namaste, beta. How are you?"

"I'm fine. How's everybody?"

"We…we are all doing okay."

Arthik detected hesitation in his father's voice.

"What is it, father?"

There was a brief pause. Arthik's stomach clenched, and he sat down. Was his mother sick? Was his sister okay?

"Please tell me what's wrong," Arthik persisted.

"It's your Dada. He's very ill," his father murmured.

A wave of guilt enveloped Arthik. His grandfather's presence had always been a part of Arthik's life. He had always been there, in the background, like a rock.

"Is he in the hospital? What happened?" Arthik asked.

"Yes, son. He is in a coma. He has a rash all over his body. Came up a few days ago on his face, and then it spread all over. We took him to the hospital yesterday."

"Should I come home, father?"

"No, beta." There was finality in his father's voice. "It would not help him. He wouldn't know you are here anyway. It's okay. You pray for him. The doctors said he doesn't have long. He has some sort of infection, though they don't know what it is. His heart is already weak because of his advanced age."

Arthik was silent. He didn't know what to say. "Do you need money?" he asked.

"No...no. We can manage. You just work hard. How's your apartment?"

"It's good, father. The work is also going well. They are nice to me here."

Arthik could hear his mother in the background.

"Your mother's asking if you are eating alright. She's worried about you," his father said.

A faint smile touched Arthik. "Tell her I'm eating a lot. Food is so easy to cook here."

"She's asking you to stay away from beef."

"Tell her not to worry. I only eat chicken and fish," Arthik said. "I'll call you in the morning. Namaste, father."

CHAPTER 7

NEXT MORNING, ARTHIK WALKED THROUGH THE
blinding rain, negotiating puddles the best he could. The umbrella
wasn't really helping much. The wind whipped the rain into his
face. It was his turn to open the office this morning. Marge would
be in later. He made it to the store at 5:55 a.m. He fumbled with
the keys for a moment.

"What a mess," he murmured as he looked at his drenched
slacks and shoes. There would be a lot of mopping today, with
customers walking in with wet shoes and clothes. He turned on
the lights and waited for the first delivery of supplies to come
in. He got a couple of dry towels from the bathroom and started
wiping the glass windows on the front of the store from the inside.
He looked out at the pouring rain, and his eyes caught a box on
the concrete pavement outside, just to the right of the door. It was
wrapped in polythene. Arthik frowned as he stared at the box
from inside the store. Had that package been there when he had

come in? Or did somebody just drop it off? He peered closely at the package again. Through the polythene, he could see a thick blue stripe running across the top of the box.

"That's Keith's package," Arthik murmured as he took quick steps to the door. Marge had told him yesterday to expect a package for their manager. He carried the package into the office in the back. It was a little heavy, probably about 30 pounds. He put it in the far corner of the room, after carefully removing the outer plastic wrap. There was no name on the box, no address or any postmarks. A blue strip of half-inch tape ran along the top of the box. This box was hand delivered to the store. Arthik turned it around. Just then, he heard the rumble of a truck pulling up in front of the store. He pushed the box against the wall and hurried to the front.

The morning went by quickly. Arthik looked at his watch. 11:30 a.m. Just then the phone rang.

"Convenience Café, how may I help you," Arthik spoke into the phone.

"Hey, Art." It was Marge.

"Hi, Marge."

"Can I talk to Keith for a second?" she said.

"Keith? Was he supposed to come in today?" Arthik said.

"You mean he's not at the store?"

"No, he hasn't been here at all."

"You've been alone all morning?" Marge asked.

"Yeah, it's been okay. Not too busy. Hold on, I got to take care of a customer."

"That's fine. I'll be there in a few minutes. Bye."

The line clicked dead. Arthik became busy again with customers waiting at the cash register. Marge walked in after a few minutes and helped him right away to clear the cluster of customers. After a while, when things became a little slow, Arthik glanced at his watch again. 12:15 p.m. He looked outside. The skies still looked angry, with no let-up in sight.

"Hey, Marge," he said. "I have to call India. My grandfather is very ill. Can I use the office to call?"

"Sure, Art," Marge said. "Hope he gets better. You can use the house phone. I'm sure Keith won't mind."

"Thank you. I'll use my cell phone." Arthik walked back to the office. He pressed his father's cell phone number.

"Namaste, father," Arthik said.

"Namaste, son."

Arthik was afraid to ask the question. "How is Dada?" he managed to get out.

"He's hanging in there. The doctors say he's stable for now."

"Has he woken up?" Arthik asked. Relief underlined his voice.

"No, beta, he's still in a coma. The doctors are not hopeful that he'll ever come out. The rest is in God's hands. The rash is really horrific. It covers his entire body. And Arthik?"

There was a brief silence.

"Yes, father. What is it?"

"Well, I hate to ask you…" His father's voice petered down.

"Tell me, father." Arthik's voice was anxious. *What is it?*

There was a short pause.

"If you could send some money?"

"Sure. I will arrange it in a couple of days. Don't worry," Arthik said.

"We would like Dada to stay here in the hospital, and it's very expensive. If we take him home, we won't be able to care for him—"

"I'm going to send you money in the next couple of days." Arthik felt less guilty now. At least he was able to do something for his family. He could borrow the money from Keith or Ajeet.

"Let me get your mother, she wanted to talk to you. She has been under the weather too for the last few days."

"Yes, father." Arthik sat on the edge of the desk. His eyes wandered to the box with a blue stripe on top. *I wonder what's in it,* Arthik thought.

"Namaste, beta," his mother's voice crackled over the wires.

"Namaste, Ma. How are you?"

"I'm okay. Are you eating well? How do you cook?"

Arthik smiled. With Ma, it was always about food. "I'm fine, Ma. Don't worry about me. You look after yourself."

As he hung up the phone, voices filtered in from the front of the store. A loud thud and a scream followed. Arthik rushed out of the room, towards the front. He stood still in shock at the scene unfolding before him. There were two men holding Marge on the customer side of the counter. Each stood on either side of her, towering above her petite figure. One of them had her head pushed down hard on the granite counter, crushing her lips between the surface and her teeth. Blood oozed from a split lip. Her eyes were wide, and fear contorted her face. Both men wore ski masks, one black and the other red, covering their faces. For a split second, Arthik didn't comprehend what was going on.

"Where's your fucking manager? Where's Keith, you bitch?" one of the masked men yelled in her ear.

Everything seemed in slow motion for Arthik. It all seemed surreal. These things were not supposed to happen in America. He stood frozen in time. The two masked men hadn't noticed him.

"Help—" Marge's scream was cut short by a fist to her face. At that instant, something snapped inside Arthik. He took a step forward. The man on Marge's left side, with the red mask, saw him and started to turn towards him.

Arthik put his hands over the counter and raised himself to go to the other side, as if on a pommel horse. As he swung over granite counter, he splayed his legs. His right foot caught the face of the man who was turning towards him. There was a cracking noise as Arthik's shoe contacted the man's jaw. The man fell over backwards on to the shelves, scattering soda cans and potato chip packets on the floor. Some of the cans popped, and fluid sprayed over the fallen man. A boxful of six-foot brooms crashed to the floor. Meanwhile Arthik landed squarely on his feet, facing the man with the black mask, who had let go of Marge and turned towards Arthik. He looked at his accomplice on the floor, writhing in pain.

"You son of a bitch! I'm going to slice you," he screamed. He pulled out a knife and advanced menacingly towards Arthik.

Arthik was in his zone now. His eyes turned to slits. He only saw his assailant now. His mind blocked off everything else. Zorawar Singh's voice boomed in his subconscious. *"You know you are going to take him down. The only question is how."*

Marge had slipped to the floor, a soft whimper emanating from her bloody lips. Arthik focused on the knife moving towards him. He swooped one of the broomsticks into his hands. He held it horizontally in front of him, tight across his chest, his arms fully extended. The assailant paused for a spilt second, eyeing the broom, not sure what to expect. After that microsecond of sanity, the eyes got crazed again.

"I'm gonna kill you, you piece of shit—" The man wearing the black ski mask screamed and lunged at Arthik.

Arthik bent his knees and stood still until the assailant was almost on top of him. He then went down on one knee and raised his arms above his shoulders, holding the broomstick firm. The assailant flailed in the air, half bent over the broomstick. Then Arthik moved his hands backwards in one single fluid motion, the broomstick flinging the assailant against the vending machine. There was a resounding crash as the glass shield of the vending machine shattered. Before the fallen man could get up, Arthik rushed up to him and brought the broomstick down on the back of his head.

The red ski masked man had gathered himself in the meantime and tackled Arthik from behind. They both went crashing down. Marge staggered to the other side of the counter and punched the emergency button.

Arthik twisted himself free from his assailant. Out of the corner of his vision, Arthik saw the black masked man struggling to get up. Arthik's mind was clear and analytical. He had about 5 seconds before they would come at him.

"You are dead…DEAD!" shouted the one in the red mask, in front of him, his left jaw at an odd angle. The ski mask now hung loose on his face.

Arthik's mind seemed to be floating above the chaos. There was no blood though, his mind noticed. The red mask was dry. That seemed odd. No blood, despite the grotesque disfigurement.

Zorawar Singh's voice echoed. "*Identify the weak spot of your opponent and make that a target.*"

The man with the disfigured jaw rushed towards him. The overhead light reflected off the knife in his right hand. Arthik took a long step and his left hand gripped the assailant's right wrist as it descended, and his right hand balled into a fist and landed an uppercut on the already damaged jaw. His fist seemed to dig halfway into the man's face, pushing the red mask deep into the hideous jaw. Blood spurted and turned the ski mask to a deeper shade of red as the skin split under the thin cloth. The assailant's eyes rolled unnaturally, and he dropped to the ground without a sound. Arthik's mind voiced approval from the subconscious depths of his long training. Now there was balance, the oozing blood made the disfigurement look real.

Now to the other scum. Arthik's expressionless face turned toward the black masked assailant, who was halfway up from the floor. Arthik took quick steps to close in the space between them and kicked him in the stomach. A quick left jab to the face was followed by a vicious right uppercut. He slumped motionless to the floor. Arthik stood over him with his fists clenched, his eyes still narrow slits. Almost hoping that the fallen man would get up, so he could hit him again, and again. Arthik seethed inside. Marge's bloody lip was still vivid.

"Is he…is he dead?" A voice floated to him.

Arthik unclenched his fists and looked at his bruised hands. He turned around slowly, as his head cleared. He saw Marge standing behind the counter, with her hands shielding her face. Her eyes were wide, her mouth half open. The wail of sirens filtered through and was getting louder. Arthik walked around the counter and held Margie. Her body shook uncontrollably. His arms tightened as he held her closer.

"Thank you," Marge said softly. "You saved my life." Her arms slipped around his waist, and she hugged him back as though she never wanted to let go.

"It's going to be okay," Arthik murmured. "You are going to be fine." *God, she smells good,* he thought.

Two patrol cars screeched to a halt outside the store. Two officers came rushing in, with drawn guns.

"Hands!" shouted one of the officers. "Hands where we can see them."

The other officer pointed his gun at the fallen men.

Margie and Arthik put their hands up.

"I punched the alert button, officer," Margie said, her voice surprisingly steady.

"What happened here? What happened to these guys?" one of them said, staring at the two men lying on the floor. He holstered his gun and turned to Margie. "I am Officer Brandon. Please put your hands down and identify yourselves."

CHAPTER 8

A COUPLE OF HOURS LATER, THE STORE WAS SETTLING again to its normal routine. Customers were trickling in. The paramedics had taped Margie's lip laceration, and the healthy glow to her cheeks returned. The rain was a drizzle now. Officer Brandon approached Arthik and Margie from the back office. He had just reviewed the footage from the store's security video cameras.

"Where did you learn to fight like that?" he asked Arthik.

"I was not fighting, Officer. I was defending myself," Arthik responded.

"Point well taken, my man. But you were awesome. It was as if I was watching a choreographed fight scene in a movie, the way you took these two down."

Arthik looked at him and just smiled. "Is that a compliment?"

"Oh, yes, it is. Did these guys ask for your manager by name?" Officer Brandon asked Margie.

"Yes, one of them did. And Keith hasn't called or come in today, which is really unusual. I have left him three messages," Margie said.

"Please have him call us when you talk to him. We will work on these two and see what happens. If anything else turns up, we'll let you know. You owe this guy one." Officer Brandon said, pointing to Arthik, who was at the counter, helping a customer.

"I know, Officer. I don't know what would have happened if Art hadn't stepped in."

"We will investigate. Whatever they were here for, Art interrupted them, and, oh boy, did he work them over," the officer said, shaking his head. "We'll have patrol cars run by here for the next few days."

"Thanks, Officer, for responding so quickly," Marge said.

"You take care now. I'll be back tomorrow."

The rest of the day went by quickly. Marge refused to go home in spite of Arthik's repeated requests.

"You sure you don't want to go home?" Arthik asked yet again.

"I'm sure, Art," Marge said, "and thanks for what you did today. I don't how it would have ended if it were not for you." She shuddered. "Maybe it doesn't make sense because this is where I was attacked, but I feel safer here, with you, and I'm just not ready to leave yet."

Arthik walked over to her and put a hand on her shoulder. "Anybody would have done the same," he said.

Margie turned around and gave him a long, tight hug. Arthik instinctively wrapped his arms around her. It seemed the natural thing to do. His heart thumped.

"You are a brave man, Art," Marge said, stepping back. She looked straight into his eyes. "You seemed to be in a different world. It was like you became a different person…a stranger."

"You don't have to be scared of me," Arthik said, looking away.

"I know," Marge said. She looked out the glass doors. "God, there's another storm coming."

Arthik followed her gaze. The skies were dark again, and there was a smattering of raindrops on the glass panels. In the next instant, it started pouring. And it came down hard. Marge put her hand on his arm.

"Have dinner with me tonight?" she asked, looking at him with an earnestness that made his stomach twist in the most pleasant way.

He tried to keep his voice calm. "Tonight?" he asked.

"Yes."

Arthik looked at her for a long moment. He reached out and held her small hands in his. The sound of rain smacking the large glass windows was deafening.

"Let me take you out," he said.

"No, I want to cook for you. Come to my place tonight," Marge said.

Arthik nodded. He was calm on the outside.

"Eight?" she asked.

Arthik nodded again.

"Good, I'll text you my address." She stood on her tiptoes and brushed her lips on his.

Arthik's heart was in his throat. He felt he could not breathe. A couple of customers walked in, bringing in the fragrance of moist vegetation and humid air. Marge smiled and walked towards the cash register. Arthik stood rooted at the spot. *Move, man, move…Arthik's mind told him. Can't keep standing here like a zombie.*

After a couple of hours, Arthik signaled to Marge that he was going to take a break. He walked back to the break room, sat down, and put his face in his hands. *What a day.*

He touched his lips with his fingers. He could still feel the sweet press of Margie's lips against his. His heart started pounding again. He shook his head and smiled like a schoolboy, knowing he would see her again this evening. Just the two of them.

He had been able to control himself. He could have hurt the two thugs more than he had. The conversation with his father reverberated in his mind. *God, that was just this morning. It seemed so long ago.* He pulled out his phone and dialed Ajeet's number.

"Hi, Ajeet, this is Art," he said. His throat hurt a bit.

"Hi, Arthik, how are you?"

"I'm okay. I have to ask a favor of you."

"Sure. What's up?"

"My grandfather is not doing well, and I need some money to pay for his care."

"I'm sorry about your grandfather. How much money do you need, Arthik?" Ajeet replied.

"Maybe a couple of thousand. I'll return it in a few months—"

"Don't worry about it. You can pick up the check this evening and wire the money tonight. All good at work?"

"Well, there was some commotion today. I'll tell you about it when I see you this evening."

"Commotion? Everything okay?"

"Yes, all is well. I am really very thankful for your help."

"You are very welcome, Arthik. I'll see you this evening. Let's have dinner together."

"Sorry, can't tonight. Can I see you around 6 p.m.?"

"Yeah, sure. See you then."

Arthik and Marge finished up their day at the store as the next shift came in to take over.

"Art, can you open the store again tomorrow? Keith still hasn't called back yet. I guess he must be caught up somewhere," Margie asked.

"Sure," Arthik replied. "His box came in, though. It's in the office."

"Oh, yeah? He gets that delivery every few weeks, and he's usually excited to see it. I'll leave him a message about it. See you later this evening then?"

"I got your text with the address. I'll be there at 8."

"Yeah, sure. Will you have trouble getting there?"

"No, I'll get a cab."

"Oh, good. I'll see you then," Margie said, her lips curving into a smile. The smile made her eyes dance.

Arthik went to see Ajeet at his workplace. His throat felt like it was on fire, and he had developed a mild cough. He had this constant tickle in his throat.

"Hi, Arthik," Ajeet said. "You look sick. You feeling all right?"

"I do feel a little sick…got a sore throat," Arthik said and promptly started coughing.

Ajeet sat him down and felt his forehead.

"You got a fever, my man," he said. "Here's your check for two thousand dollars. Grab Advil on your way out and make sure you see a doctor tomorrow."

"Thank you for the check, Ajeet," Arthik said. "I don't have a doctor."

"I'll make an appointment for you for tomorrow morning to see my doctor," Ajeet said. "You going home now?"

"Yes, and…." Arthik stopped.

"And what?" Ajeet asked.

"I am going to Marge's house at eight," Arthik replied. His face turned red.

"Good for you, Arthik," Ajeet said, smiling ear to ear. "Make sure you take a couple of Advils now. And take a nice bottle of wine and flowers. Okay?"

"Uh huh," Arthik said as he hurried away, his face still burning.

Arthik was at Marge's door promptly at 8 p.m. and rang the bell. His hands gripped the wine bottle and the bouquet. His throat was still hurting, especially when he coughed.

"Hi, Art," Marge said as she stood in the doorway, welcoming him in.

For a long moment, Arthik could not speak. Marge wore a tight red dress, accentuating her curves. Strands of ash blond hair caressed her forehead. The smile lit up her face in a thousand different ways. Her right upper lip was still swollen.

"You look very beautiful," Arthik blurted out. "I…I've never seen you in regular clothes." He handed her the flowers and the bottle of wine.

"Thanks, Art, that is so sweet of you. You are just in time… dinner's ready," Marge said.

Time flew quickly. Arthik loosened up after a glass of wine. The conversation flowed freely. After dinner, they both flopped on the couch in the living room.

"So where are you from in India?" Marge asked.

"Punjab, in North India. What do you know about India?" Arthik asked.

"Nothing more than what I've heard from you." Marge smiled.

"It's a different world out there," Arthik said, staring into his wine glass.

"You miss India, don't you?" Marge said, running her hand through his thick hair.

"I do," Arthik replied, pulling her closer. There was no nervousness now. He felt comfortable, as if he had known Marge for a long time. "Did you grow up in this area?" he continued.

"No. I'm from Minot, North Dakota," she replied, resting her head on his shoulder.

"North Dakota? Isn't that very cold?" Arthik asked.

"Yes, it's very cold, but with a warm heart," she replied.

"And beautiful girls," Arthik said. His lips curved into a faint smile.

"Hmm…." Marge snuggled closer and shut her eyes.

"The food was so delicious," Arthik said, and started to cough. Suddenly, his throat pain seemed to have worsened.

"You are coughing and your face is burning up. You feeling okay?"

"I have a sore throat, but it's not that bad," Arthik said. He didn't sound convincing, even to himself.

Marge put her hand on his forehead.

"You have a fever," she said. "I'm going to get you some Advil. I can take you to an urgent care tonight."

"No…no. I have a doctor's appointment tomorrow at 11. As much as I don't want to, I'd better leave now," Arthik said.

"Nonsense. I'm not letting you go home. You stay here tonight." Marge's tone was final.

"Stay here? No, I can't—"

"Oh, don't be a prude. This sofa is a pull-out bed. I'll rig up some blankets. And don't worry about opening the store in the morning. I'll take care of that."

Arthik realized he felt too sick and exhausted to argue. The alcohol was getting to him. He could barely keep his eyes open.

Arthik felt worse in the morning when he woke up. His throat felt like glass needles were poking on the inside. For a second he did not realize where he was. Then the last evening came rushing back. He looked around, but had difficulty seeing anything as it was still dark outside. Across the room, he could see a light was on under the bedroom door. He took off the blankets covering him and sat up on the sofa bed. He was still in his jeans and T-shirt. His mouth had that familiar sick-breath smell. He willed himself to stand up and staggered to the kitchen sink. He splashed cold water on his face.

"You are up early," Marge's voice rang out behind him. "How are you feeling?"

"Not that great," Arthik turned around. She looked radiant, wrapped up in a pink bathrobe and wearing a big smile, as usual. "Thanks for letting me stay here last night."

"Of course. It's the least I could do to take care of you after you saved me yesterday. Here's a towel."

"Thank you." Arthik wiped his face. "What time is it?" he asked.

"5:30. I made breakfast for us," she replied.

"Thanks. Can you drop me home on the way to the store?" he asked.

"Sure. You want me to take you to the doctor's office later?" Marge asked.

"You'll be busy in the store. I'll manage." Arthik wrapped her in his arms and held her close. "Thank you for everything. If I wasn't sick, I would kiss you long and hard," he said, with a smile that touched his eyes.

"Hmm…is that right?" she replied with a soft smile.

"You can bet on it," Arthik said.

"Then get well *real* soon," Marge replied with a grin and gave him a quick peck on his cheek.

The Advil kept Arthik going, and he took a Loudoun County Transit bus to get to the doctor's office in Lansdowne.

"I don't have insurance," Arthik said to the receptionist at the doctor's office.

"That's okay, Mr. Sharma. Please fill out these new patient forms, and Dr. Singh will see you in a few minutes."

Arthik filled out the required paperwork and was escorted to an exam room a few minutes later.

After a brief wait, the doctor walked in. He was probably in his early forties, about five feet seven inches tall, dark and extremely fit. His clothes matched his athletic build.

"Hi, Arthik, I'm Dr. Karnail Singh. So what brings you here today?"

"Thanks for seeing me at such short notice. I've a sore throat and fever, which seems to be getting worse."

"Let's take a quick look. Does your throat hurt when you swallow?"

"Yeah, Doctor, it does."

The doctor was quick and extremely thorough in his exam.

"You have a throat infection. I'll write an antibiotic for you. Drink lots of fluids, and you should be good in a couple of days."

"If you don't mind, Doctor, please write an inexpensive one. I am really hard up on cash."

Dr. Singh looked up at him for a moment.

"Don't worry, Arthik. I'll see if I have any samples."

"Thanks, Doc, and please call me Art."

Dr. Singh looked at him again, this time for a long moment. A slight smile touched his face.

"How long have you been in this country, Arthik?" Dr. Singh asked.

Arthik thought there was an emphasis on his name.

"About a year, Doc," he replied.

Dr. Singh rubbed his chin momentarily and looked at him again.

"I have been here 25 years. You know the most important thing I realized after all these years?"

Arthik looked at him and shrugged.

"Never, ever forget your roots," Dr. Singh smiled. "Your name is the first gift your parents gave you. Try not to mangle it. I'll get your antibiotic now."

As Dr. Singh walked out of the exam room, Arthik tried to digest what he had just heard.

A physician and a philosopher.

CHAPTER 9

THE NEXT MORNING, ARTHIK WOKE UP EARLY TO GET to the store. His throat felt a lot better with the antibiotic. The morning was busy and flew by quickly. Marge arrived for work at noon, came up to him, and gave him a tight hug. Arthik hugged back. It seemed the natural thing to do.

"You doing okay, Marge?" Arthik asked, searching her face. The lip looked a lot better.

"Yeah, Art, I'm doing well. Thanks to you. How about you?"

"I'm fine. Just worried about my folks back home. My grandfather is not doing well at all."

"I'm sorry to hear that," Margie said. "Did you call home today?"

"No, not yet." Arthik looked at his watch. "Actually, this is a good time to call. Mind if I go back and take a couple minutes?"

"Not at all. You take your time."

Arthik went into the back office and dialed his father's number. There was no answer. *Maybe he is at the hospital visiting grandfather. I'll call in a few minutes,* he thought to himself. He put his head back and shut his eyes. The last couple of days muddled through his brain. He rubbed his face and hung his head in his hands. And where the hell was Keith? The man had not shown up or called in two days.

The assailants had repeatedly asked for him. Maybe he was in trouble. That box! Keith's delivery package was right there in the room. Arthik got to his feet and stepped to the far corner and stood over the box. For a moment, he had qualms about opening Keith's package, but only for a brief second. He peeled off the tape and opened the box. There was a sheet of polythene on top. Arthik lifted the polythene and let out an audible gasp. There was a layer of neatly stacked Ziplock bags, each packed with $100 bills. Arthik did not move for what seemed an eternity. He lost track of time. He just could not take his eyes off the box of money. Benjamin Franklin stared back at him, through the plastic. He bent down slowly, and picked up one of the Ziploc bags and examined it closely. It felt heavy in his palm. His hands dove back into the box, and there were layers and layers of the packages, neatly stacked on top of each other. *This is real,* he thought to himself. *There must be thousands, maybe hundreds of thousands?*

God!

He did not know how much money was staring back at him. He was only sure that it was a lot. He put the packet back in the box and put the blue tape back on to seal the box. With his heart pounding, Arthik paced up and down the confines of the small room. Should he tell Marge? He almost jumped out of his skin as his cell phone buzzed. It was his father calling from India.

"Hello father. How is everything?"

"Not well, son," his father replied. Arthik detected a quiver in his voice. "Your grandfather died this morning."

Arthik felt an empty hole in his gut. He sat down and ran his hand through his hair.

"I'm so sorry, father. How is everybody holding up?" Arthik was surprised at how calm he sounded.

"That rash...the rash your grandfather had. We all have it. Your mother has it the worst. And we are all coughing. Half the village has it, we are all very sick. They are saying terrorists spread a virus. I'm scared, Arthik." His voice trailed off, as he started coughing.

Arthik's brain could not comprehend what he had just heard. He could not speak for a few seconds. He felt suffocated. It was as if someone had sucker-punched him. He took a deep breath as helplessness consumed him. This was the first time he had ever heard his father sound weak and vulnerable.

"Arthik? Are you there?"

"I'm here, father. Did you go to the doctor?" Arthik's voice was controlled. Almost mechanical.

"The local doctor died this morning. I heard a few other people have died in the village. All of them had this rash. The Indian Army is here—"

"Army? I'm coming home, father. I'll be on the next flight out."

"No...no. Do not come here. We are glad you are safe. The Army is here now...they will look after us."

Arthik was quiet for a moment. His eyes wandered over to the box with the blue stripe. That sinking feeling persisted. But he knew exactly what he had to do. In those few seconds, his mind laid out a clear path for him.

"I'm coming home, father. You hang in there. Get the best treatment available. Don't worry about money. I wired you one lakh rupees yesterday. You borrow from whoever. I'll bring enough money."

Arthik walked up to the front of the store. His heart was heavy, but his mind was crystal clear.

"Hey, Marge, I am going to India tomorrow. My grandfather died this morning." Arthik was matter-of-fact.

"Oh…I am so sorry, Art," Marge said, her hand covering her mouth. She walked to him and hugged him. Arthik held her for a long moment. His arms were stiff.

"Thanks, Marge. I know it'll be tough here, but I don't have a choice."

"Don't worry about the store. I'll get temp help. Family first. Always. The store will still be here when you get back. How are your folks holding up?"

"They are all sick. The whole village has this weird rash. People are dying." Arthik's voice trailed off.

Margie's hug instinctively got tighter.

"I'm so sorry, Art. I wish I could do something for you. Go home and start packing. Be safe."

"I'll get my stuff together and go out the back door. You take care of yourself," Arthik said.

Arthik walked back to the office and shut the door. He picked up a small trash bag and transferred some of the money packets from the box. There were no qualms, just clarity of purpose. He then sealed the box back again.

CHAPTER 10

RAYMOND COLLING DROVE SLOWLY TOWARDS HIS office on 10th Street in Washington, DC. He had not slept last night since he received the text from Dr. Blakely, his immediate superior at the Institute for Prevention of Biological Warfare.

It had simply read, "XT4 ? active." It was finally happening. But he had to play normal. There could not be any misstep. He had not replied to the text. He was not supposed to. There were servers where text messages could stick for an uncomfortably long time.

Ever since the passing of his wife five years ago, Colling had devoted himself to his work. All his plans of retiring to their beach house in California had disappeared when his wife died a sudden, unexpected death.

Colling's life as he knew it, had come to an abrupt end at that time. The world suddenly became stark and cold. He was angry and bitter that, except for him, nobody else cared that he was alone. The world had not missed a beat as his life had come to a grinding halt. The bitterness and anger took over his being. From the depth of his soul, he wanted to get back at the world for its callousness. They did not have any children, and neither he, nor his wife, had any family to speak of. He had become a recluse, shuttling between his lab and his administrative office. His circle of friends dwindled as he became socially inert. Nearing 60, his work was all he cared for and was his entire life now.

Waiting at a traffic light, he pulled out his phone and looked at that text again. The "XT4" jumped at him, like it had numerous times since last night. The XT4 was the deadliest virus the world would ever know. And Raymond Colling's knowledge of it was not to be taken lightly. He was a double PhD from Stanford, in Immunology and Microbiology & Entomology.

His dissertation, "*Microbes that can end Civilization*" was revolutionary and had attracted the attention of the Director of the Institute for Prevention of Biological Warfare. The extremely generous compensation package had been hard to refuse. He had started working there right after earning his PhD. The freedom to do whatever he wanted had kept him there. The initial trials on animals exposed to the XT4 virus both excited and terrified him.

He drove to his designated parking slot. He did nothing out of the routine. His movements and his pace were measured. No quick steps, no hurried walking. These things had been drilled into their brains.

"*In case of an unforeseen, unexpected, or unusual event, life at the Institute is to be normal, even more normal than a normal day.*"

Colling walked through the metal detectors, and into the foyer of the innocuous-looking office building in the heart of Washington, DC. He got into the elevators and didn't bother to punch the floor number. Because these elevators only went to the tenth floor, no matter what number you punched. He looked at the mirrors lining the elevator cabin. The abnormally large, round, thick-lensed glasses stared back at him. He straightened his stooped shoulders and tried to smooth the wrinkles on his navy-blue jacket, without much success. The elevator doors opened to a narrow corridor that took Colling to a small area with three retinal scan machines. These were state of the art, and the retinal scan was completed in three seconds. Colling then walked through the reinforced steel doors. The appearance was like any corporate office. There were about 15 individual offices in the vast open floor, with smaller cubicles spread in between.

Colling nodded to his secretary as he entered his office.

"Good morning, Claire. Any messages for me?" He had to keep up appearances. Claire did not have the security clearance to know about what could be going on.

"Good morning, Dr. Colling. The chief's office called. He asked you to stop by whenever you have a moment. Nothing urgent," she said. "A few papers to sign and your letters are on your desk."

"Thanks," Colling murmured and walked into his office. He spent the next 30 minutes just signing paperwork and going through routine motions. The 30 minutes seemed like hours. Finally, he buzzed the intercom.

"Claire, please check if Dr. Blakely has a few minutes now."

"Sure, Dr. Colling."

After a minute, Colling walked into his superior's office. Blakely stood by the window, gazing outward, tall and silent. He waved Colling to a chair.

Colling sat down and waited. The silence was heavy for a few seconds.

"I thought the XT4 was pulled out of all labs, Raymond," Blakely finally said, his face a scowl.

Colling processed the statement for a second before replying. "As far as I know, it has been," he said. Denial was the best defense here.

Blakely walked back to his desk. He put his arms on the table and leaned forward, his face inches from Colling's. "Are you being clean with me, Raymond?" he hissed.

"Yes, Dr. Blakely, I am. Can you please tell me what is going on?" This time Colling did not pause or flinch even for a nano second. He had to sound convincing.

Blakely stared at him for a moment and then pushed himself back. He took a deep breath and sat down across the table.

"There seems to be an outbreak around one of the lab facilities," he said, his voice just a little more than a whisper.

Colling felt his heart racing. "Outbreak? What do you mean?" he asked.

"Exposure, contamination, infection. I don't know. People are dying. Innocent people, children. A whole village." Blakely's voice trailed off.

Colling pretended to freeze for a moment. "It's not possible. Are you sure?" Colling said.

"The symptoms are exactly like you said they would be, if there was a person to person transmission." Blakely's voice was a notch higher now.

"But there is no human to human transmission so far. There isn't even a documented human infection. Despite our efforts to infect that remote tribe—"

"Keep your goddamned voice down, dammit." Blakely dabbed his forehead with tissues to wipe away the sweat. "Our intel points to the lab in Pakistan, with infection in a neighboring village in India. Maybe some rogue ISI agents or a terrorist outfit. It's sketchy at this point."

Colling was silent. This was not the way it was supposed to happen.

"How could this happen? We have the virus isolated in a lab. There is no known animal host or carrier. Unless…" His voice was a whisper. "Unless the virus mutated." His eyes gleamed as he rubbed his hands.

"I told you a hundred times, Raymond. Never weaponize a virus before you have a vaccine. But you didn't listen. You carried on with your research."

Colling blanked him out. There was no point in arguing. Blakely was weak. There was a bigger purpose in all of this. He stood up and looked straight at Blakely.

"What is done cannot be undone," Colling said. The look in his eyes kept Blakely quiet. "First we make sure that it is XT4. If it is, we must find out the mode of transmission, and if there is any animal carrier. At least we know that it is a potent virus. This can be used in the future for our defense."

"Defense? *Defense?!*" Blakely almost yelled.

Colling stepped in front of Blakely and pointed his index finger at him, an inch from his face. "Don't mess this up more than what it already is. Keep it together," Colling said, his voice soft, almost caressing. "If you don't, I promise on my wife's grave, I will end your sniveling, miserable life. You get it?"

Blakely felt the menace in Colling's voice and took a quick step back, looking away.

"Look at me," Colling said, his voice sharper now.

Blakely took another step back. Colling moved with surprising agility and hooked his arm around his neck, pulling Blakely's face inches from his own.

"You get it, Dr. Blakely?" Colling hissed.

Blakely's eyes opened wide. He felt Colling's coffee breath on his face. Sweat poured down his face.

"I…I get it, Raymond. Cool it, man, I'm with you. You handle this. We'll do whatever you want. XT4 is your creation, it's your baby," Blakely managed to get out.

Colling's breath was heavy for a moment, and then he loosened his grip. He stepped back and patted Blakely's cheek, and then straightened his neck tie.

"I'm glad we are on the same page, Dr. Blakely. Route all contact from the NSA and CDC to me. I'll take it from here," Colling said, speaking slowly, and then he abruptly walked out of the room.

Blakely swallowed hard as he watched him walk out.

Colling stared out the window at the Washington Monument from his desk. It was a clear day, and the monument looked majestic. He had to protect this country from terrorists. It was all up to him and people like him. People who would not flinch to cross the line on occasion for the greater good. Bureaucrats like Blakely were spineless paper pushers. He stood up and walked to the small window and caught his reflection on the glass. A middle-aged man, about 5 feet 10 inches tall, with a shock of unkempt white hair stared back at him. Age and bitterness had crinkled his facial skin, and he looked much older than his 58 years. He shook his head and ran his hand through his hair.

He had to take the next step. He just had to. The XT4 program had to survive. The virus had to live, to kill another day. He pulled out his cell and punched a number.

"Hello, this is Roger Clifton," a brisk voice replied.

"This is Dr. Colling. From the IPBW."

Silence spun down the wire for a couple of seconds.

"Where did you get this number?" Clifton was being cautious.

"From Dr. Blakely."

"Where is he?"

"Indisposed. I'm it now," Colling said, his voice firm.

There was another short silence.

"What did you need, Raymond?" Clifton's voice finally came down.

Raymond? So, Clifton knew about him. He kept quiet.

"It's about this outbreak in Northern India, isn't it?" Clifton continued.

"I can't talk about this on the phone. We need to meet," Colling said.

"When?" Clifton asked.

"Yesterday."

Another silence, but much shorter.

"Carly's café, corner of 7th and H. Thirty minutes." The line clicked dead.

Colling was at the café in less than half an hour. He sat at a corner table and waited. He knew he was being watched. Clifton probably had eyes on him since the second he stepped out of his office. The Agency was good at this. He knew that at this time, Clifton knew as much about him as there was to know. But there was one thing nobody could ever know. They could check his credit cards, his assets, his credentials, his published scientific papers, his research, and so many other things. But there was no technology that could peek into the depths of his soul to measure the bitterness that resided there. Colling ordered a coffee and waited.

After about 15 minutes, a middle-aged African American man in a dapper suit slid into the chair in front of him.

"Raymond Colling?" he asked.

Colling recognized the voice. He nodded and held out his hand. "Yes, Mr. Clifton. How are you?"

"What's up, Doctor? What is the emergency?" Clifton's voice was impatient.

"Are you wearing a wire?" Colling asked.

"What? Are you serious?" Clifton's face was a scowl.

"Mr. Clifton, please listen to me carefully. I am going to say this only once. The reason I don't want you to record this conversation is to give you plausible deniability later, if the shit hits the fan. Do you understand me?" Colling's voice had steel in it.

Clifton looked at him for a long second, and then ran his hand through his sparse hair.

"No, I am not wearing a wire, Dr. Colling. I am all ears."

"Are you familiar with the XT4 program?" Colling asked.

"Yes, I am," Clifton replied, looking around. The closest person to them was four tables away. "It was an attempt to weaponize viruses. Was scrapped four years ago. It was considered too dangerous, and very unethical. Biological warfare makes a lot of folks uneasy," he continued in a low voice.

"You are correct, but not entirely," Colling said.

Clifton's eyebrows seemed to merge in a frown. "What do you mean?"

"The XT4 was not scrapped entirely. The outbreak in India is XT4," Colling said quietly.

Clifton became very still. "XT4 was scrapped. I saw the file before I came here." His voice was barely above a whisper now.

"The operation was active at five centers. Four of them were scrapped, but not in Western Pakistan." Colling was enjoying himself now. He reveled in seeing other people cringe in fear.

"Under whose authority?"

"By people who are at a much higher pay grade than both of us, so that is classified. I don't know who authorized the whole operation, but the money flowed freely."

Clifton's mouth was half open. One could almost feel the frantic activity that was going on in his brain.

"From what I know, the reason it was scrapped was that if the virus mutated and there was human to human transmission, it would be impossible to control. There's no vaccine. Millions will die." Clifton's voice was barely above a whisper. He folded his hands together and swallowed.

"You have to think of the bigger picture," Colling said sharply, his voice laced with contempt. "You wipe these terrorists off the face of the earth. And let there be peace and tranquility after that."

A vein became prominent on Clifton's forehead. His eyes blazed. "Are you fucking listening to yourself? You are out of your mind. Once this virus spreads, it's not going to discriminate between good and evil. I am going to put a stop to this right now," and he started to get up.

"Sit down." The ice in Colling's voice froze Clifton. He hesitated for a second, and then sat again. "If this goes public, we all, and I stress *we*—including you and anybody else ever involved in this program—we all go down." Colling paused and let the words sink in.

Clifton stared at his hands for a few seconds. "How are you sure this outbreak is XT4?" His voice was even toned and controlled again.

"I am not. But it sure looks like it. I still don't know how the population got infected. But the way I see it now, it will be self-limiting." Colling's lip curved into a hint of a smile.

"Self-limiting? How?" Clifton ignored the smile.

"The disease is so severe that eventually it will start killing people before they can spread the disease." Colling's voice was soft, almost caressing. "But the virus has to be recovered. We just have to get it."

"It has to be destroyed. Nobody should have it," Clifton said.

"Don't be foolish. XT4 will be like a nuclear weapon. It will be a deterrent. We must have it," Colling said. "Once we have it, we can research it more, we can work on developing a vaccine."

"You are taking a big risk. This could mean the end of the world as we know it today," Clifton said.

"It's exciting, isn't it? This bug will put these fucking terrorists where they belong," Colling said, barely able to contain himself.

"Unless they have it too. They would have no qualms about using it any time, at any place," Clifton said quietly.

"That's exactly the reason we have to get somebody on the CDC team that will be flying there in a day or two. And this person will report to me." Colling's tone left no room for negotiations.

Clifton thought for a moment. "I have somebody who is good."

"What's his name?" Colling asked.

"McKay. His name is Bill McKay. He has done some contract work for your institution before."

CHAPTER 11

DR. JOHN ETERS WAS RUSHING. HE ALWAYS HATED IT when that happened. He just did not like to rush. Early this morning, he had received a call from his immediate superior at the CDC.

"Come to Room 2000 as soon as you can," Dr. Roberts had said. He was terse.

"Yes, Dr. Roberts," he had replied, half asleep. His eyes focused on his bedside clock. 4.30 a.m.

"Make it quick." The line clicked to silence.

Room 2000 was not good news. It generally meant there was an undocumented, unconfirmed outbreak somewhere. With the recent spate of terrorist events and threats, everybody was on edge. It would be the same procedure and protocol, as always. An investigative team would fly out to the site. A thorough investigation would ensue, and the primary site would be sealed off from the world. People exposed would be tested, cultured, and treated if necessary. But John hoped it was a hoax, like so many other potential attacks earlier this month. He took a quick shower and peeked inside the refrigerator before heading out. He swore under his breath as he saw the empty shelves. He splashed some juice in a cup and hurried out of his townhome to his car.

John did not want to be the last one in. He was sure the whole team had been called in. Dr. Jason Roberts was as close to being a perfectionist as one could be. He was meticulous in every little detail. With the events of the last few months as they had been, he had kept the field team at the CDC on its toes. That was precisely the reason he was one of the Deputy Directors and strongly tipped to succeed the current director when his term expired. John respected him, but wished he would lighten up a little. Until a few years ago, people all over the country were supremely confident, with an aura of invincibility and a gentle arrogance. Now there was uncertainty and a stark realization of vulnerability. But so far, people had hung on tenaciously. There was hope and belief that the law enforcement agencies would always come out on top. And so far, they had been up to the task and more. Every lead was being followed and investigated.

John and his team had worked diligently over the last few months. They had traveled at a moment's notice without any complaints. There had been no requests for time off, no complaints of sickness or exhaustion. They were, in essence, the front line of the CDC. They were the first responders to a contaminated or infected area, looking more like astronauts than scientists in their protective gear. John hoped today's call was another one of those numerous false alarms.

Atlanta in August was humid and oppressive. John raced along Peach Tree Boulevard to the CDC headquarters.

"What a life," he cursed under his breath. Never had he imagined that he would be whizzing around in his car at pre-dawn hours because of the specialty he had chosen. He had breezed through pre-med and medical school. He was considered to be one of the smartest minds in his med school. But hard work was not his forte. That was not to say he shirked work. He just did what he had to, nothing more or less. Residency in Internal Medicine was a lot of physical work. With his brilliant mind, he had no problems academically. He could have walked into any Fellowship program at the university. He surprised a lot of his friends and the faculty when he chose the relatively sedate specialty of Infectious Diseases. That was what John had always wanted to do. He was awed by the fact that microscopic organisms, whether they be bacteria or viruses, could bring the vital organs of a healthy human being to a grinding halt. History is replete with examples where seemingly unconquerable armies of invincible emperors were defeated not by their enemies, but by disease. John was an avid student of history of medicine, and these facts fascinated him.

He had joined the CDC because he wanted to be involved in research and development of new techniques to combat the ever-emerging threat of resistant bacteria and viruses. He loved the hours too—in at 8 a.m. and out at 5 p.m. But that was then, in the good old days. John sighed as he sped on. Times had changed dramatically. Ever since the bio-terrorism scare had changed into a distinct reality, things had been hectic at the CDC, to put it mildly.

Along with the increased work came tremendous responsibility. One seemingly inconsequential misstep could result in innocent people dying. The pressure on the people working on the field teams was monumental. John Eters headed one such team. He was considered one of the best field operatives, because of his vast knowledge about the theoretical aspects of Infectious Diseases, combined with his extreme analytical and practical approach to problems at a contaminated site.

John parked in his reserved slot, one of the privileges bestowed by the CDC after a few years. He half-ran, half-walked to Room 2000. It was almost 6 a.m. He knocked softly on the door and slid in. A presentation was going on in the dark room. He sat on the nearest empty seat.

"Hi," whispered a voice next to him.

He recognized the voice instantly. It belonged to Richard Kostovo, the microbiologist in his field team. John squinted at him, his eyes not yet adjusted to the darkness.

"Hi, Rich, what's this all about?" he whispered back.

"A hot zone in India—" started Rich.

"Which place in Indiana?" interrupted John quietly, very familiar with the state.

"India. Wake up, John," hissed Rich.

"A hot zone in India? Why are we involved? Why not our team in Singapore?" whispered a surprised John.

A 'hot zone' was an area with fatalities from a yet unknown infection, whether it be viral or bacterial.

"I don't know. Listen," Rich murmured.

But John could not concentrate on the speaker. He had bitter-sweet memories associated with that part of the world. About eight years ago, during his post-doctoral training at the University of Maryland, he had been involved in an intense relationship with a vivacious microbiologist. The person in question was Rupani Kapoor, a research associate from India. The relationship had been both physical and emotional. But after a couple of years, they drifted apart. Rupani had wanted more commitment from John, but at that time he was not ready for a long-term relationship. She had moved back to India at the end of her research project. John had been in a couple of relationships since then, but he had always missed Rupani. He never tried to get in touch with her in India, and he always regretted that. For him, she was the proverbial "*one that got away*." The heartache remained, after all these years. He shook his head slowly, and floated back to the present. He made an effort to hear what the speaker was saying.

The speaker was from the Pentagon and was finishing up giving the geographical and topographical details about North India. Lights came on as he concluded his presentation. Dr. Jason Roberts got up from his seat and walked over to John and Richard.

"Hi, John."

"Hi, Dr. Roberts, I am sorry I was late—" started John.

"You are fine, John. So far, these guys have been familiariz-ing us with the lay of the land. The important part begins now. Pay close attention. This might be serious. We will meet after the briefing." He sounded worried.

John and Rich settled in their seats, as the next speaker started. There were about 20 people in the room, including visitors who were distinguishable by their crisp uniforms and shiny medals.

"I am Colonel Peters from the NSA," started the new speaker. "We have identified a hot zone in northern India, about 200 miles north of New Delhi. Reports are still coming in. What we have so far is that residents of three villages in that area have been affected by a mysterious illness. The unconfirmed tally of fatalities is about 300, three days after the onset of symptoms."

Colonel Peters paused, seemingly still in shock because of the numbers that he had rattled off. He had the complete and undivided attention of every person in the room now.

John's fists clenched until his knuckles were white. *Three hundred people in three days.* He felt his stomach tighten. He wanted to know the symptoms these unfortunate people had before they died. He knew that information was coming next. There was total silence, all eyes transfixed on Colonel Peters.

"The initial presentation resembles a flu-like syndrome, followed in a few hours by a pustular rash over the entire body. This is followed by multi-system organ failure because of hemorrhagic necrosis in the next twenty-four hours. Any questions so far?"

The silence in the room was deafening. Staffers of the CDC had a general look of stunned disbelief on their faces. The only thing John could hear was his heart pounding.

"Do we have any culture results, gram stains from the lesions?" John asked hesitantly, his voice reflecting disbelief.

Colonel Peters looked at John as he asked the question.

"From the info that we have so far, nothing has grown on cultures. Gram stains are inconclusive, which hints at a virus. But it's still early. We do have some pictures."

He signaled to one of his associates, and the screen lit up behind him. The pictures depicted the dead and dying. John felt bile rising up in his throat. The unfortunate victims were of varying ages and belonged to both sexes. Some of the faces were unrecognizable because of the fulminant pustular rash that covered the entire body, including the face. The disease did not seem to spare any section of the population.

"I think the pictures speak for themselves," Colonel Peters said. His voice was flat. He gathered his papers and stepped away.

A tall, well-built man in a dark suit then got up.

"I am Alex Ricardo, with the NSA. As you all realize, this is very disconcerting. We have not identified the bacteria or virus yet. You people are experts, and we need your help." He paused for a second and then continued. "WHO has already sent a team there to try to identify and contain any further spread of the outbreak. They will work with the local authorities. The Indian Army is out there, handling security and logistics. We don't know how all this started. Could it be bioterrorism? It seems unlikely that any terrorist group would want to target a couple of small villages in India. At the same time, we want to be sure that this scenario is not taken advantage of by terrorist organizations. If they are able to get hold of this bacteria or virus, God knows what they will do with it." He was silent for a few long seconds, to let the words sink in.

"The President is aware of the situation and feels this outbreak could be a potential threat to national security. He wants a team from the CDC to go there and identify the source of this outbreak. If we can identify and culture the organism, then there is a possibility of treatment and vaccinations. Dr. Roberts will assemble a team, and we leave tonight," Ricardo concluded.

Lights came on, but none of the CDC staffers moved. John consciously uncurled his fists. He still could not digest what they had all seen and heard. This was the big one. His gut knew it. This is what people at the CDC had nightmares about. Bioterrorism or not, this outbreak had the potential for global implications.

The visitors filed out of the room.

"Come closer, all of you," Dr. Roberts said. He gave each one a thick folder. "This folder has all the info…whatever is available so far. I can't even begin to speculate what this darn outbreak is from. Any ideas?"

There was a momentary silence.

"The outbreak seems to be a combination of Ebola and smallpox. And that's not possible….," John said, his voice trailing off.

"I don't know what's going on. But I do know we realize more than anybody else how serious and disastrous this could be. I am going to ask for volunteers on this one. We need a field team with all the support staff. Go through this folder and we meet here again in one hour," Dr. Roberts said.

Everybody dispersed and started to move out of the room.

"You want to grab a bite?" Richard Kostovo asked John.

"Oh, yeah…sure, I am starving," John replied.

"So John, you up to this trip?"

"I don't know. That was a surprise. I mean Roberts asking for volunteers."

"Yeah, caught me off guard too. He is a good guy. This is going to be a long, hard trip. How long is the flight to India anyway?"

"Seventeen hours flying time with a break in between in Europe," John replied succinctly.

"Wow. How do you know that? Have you been to that part of the world?" Richard asked, taken aback by the quick answer.

"No, never been there. Just some general knowledge," John replied quickly. He still vividly remembered his conversations with Rupani about the long, tiring flights to India.

"I am impressed, Dr. Eters. So, are you going to volunteer? Roberts would love it if you do."

"I don't know yet. How about you?" John asked.

"I'll probably go. Nothing to do here, anyway," Richard replied, a bachelor and ever ready to explore new places.

Both picked up trays at the cafeteria. As they munched their food, they flipped through the folder.

John suddenly lost his appetite as he went through the material, especially the pictures. Richard was not eating much either.

"Man, what is this bug?" John exclaimed, his curiosity aroused by this mysterious affliction.

"Let's get there and check it out, John," Richard said.

John looked up, struck by the tone of Richard's voice. For a fleeting moment, he thought Richard was indulging in light banter, as he often did. But the look on his face was resolute.

"We should go. You are the best darn field team leader we have. Let's get there and beat this disease," Richard continued, his voice somber.

John looked at him for a long moment. He had known how sincere Richard was about his work. This just cemented his impression.

"Thanks for the compliment, Rich," John replied, with a smile. "Let's go lick this sucker."

"Good. Let's get back to 2000 then."

They both walked back to Room 2000. Dr. Roberts was already there.

"What's the word, guys?" he asked.

"We'll roll, boss. When does the bus leave?" John said.

"Count me in too," Richard said.

"Good," Jason Roberts said, relief pouring out of his voice. "I'll make sure the equipment is ready. You need to get your passports to me before 4 p.m. today. A State Department team is already here to do the necessary paperwork. Travel very light. It's going to be warm there and very humid. Everybody starts on malaria prophylaxis today. You should be good on all other vaccines."

All CDC field operatives remained current on all available vaccines and immigration paperwork, precisely for situations like the present one.

The equipment that Dr. Roberts was talking about was extensive and state of the art. It included lab equipment, protective gear, sophisticated investigative tools and telecommunication systems to contact headquarters in an instant.

"There will be a plane waiting at the Hartsfield International for departure at 8 p.m. tonight. The team will gather here at four and will be briefed by the State Department. You will leave directly from here to the airport. Questions?" Roberts asked.

"No. I am fine," John said, taken aback by the detailed plans.

"Okay, chief, we will see you here at four," Richard said.

CHAPTER 12

JOE KRANKEN'S ARM JERKED AS THE PHONE BUZZED
on the metal casing of his ice-box, sounding off a rattle and shattering the tranquility of a picturesque scene. Ocean waves lapped up the side of his boat.

"Damn," he swore to himself. Who in the hell was calling him? A selective few had this number. He jammed his fishing pole onto the rack on the boat railing and squinted his eyes at the caller ID. He swore again as he answered.

"Goddamn it, Gordo, I am retired," Joe barked into the phone.

"And a very good morning to you too," the voice on the other side replied. "How is Grenada?"

"You are still keeping tabs on me? You should have better things to take care of, Gordo. You being a super spy and all that—"

"Jokes apart, Joe, I need you on this one."

"No, Gordo, I am done. Retired and having a great time."

"Just hear me out—"

"Get somebody else to do your dirty work, Gordo," Kranken said, his voice oozing fatigue from all his missions over the years. "This one is different." Gordo's tone had changed. The banter was gone. "If this situation gets out of hand, our future is obliterated. And you get paid whatever you want."

There was heavy silence for a few long seconds.

"I'm listening," Kranken said, straightening up. A plane flew over the horizon, casting a reflection on the clear, calm waters of the Atlantic Ocean.

"A bug has wiped out a village in the northern part of India in three days. Three hundred people dead. And all we know is that it's some kind of virus."

Kranken's stomach clenched. "Somebody planted the bug?"

"We don't know yet. It would need a very sophisticated setup to grow, transport, and spread a virus that needs a live host. But…." Gordo went quiet.

"But what?" Kranken asked.

"There was some chatter in Southeast Asia, about something going to happen. We don't know if it was about this kind of event."

A few long seconds ticked.

"So now we are worried, considering India's geographic location. If this virus or bug falls into the wrong hands, it could cause havoc anywhere. Especially if we don't have time to develop a vaccine." Kranken's tone was deliberate, measured.

"You got it, Joe. You will have complete access. You will not belong to any agency. We must ensure that the viral cultures don't fall into the wrong hands. You are not bound by any protocols, rules, or laws."

"How high does this go, Gordo?" Kranken was curious.

He heard labored breathing on the other end. Kranken visualized a typical scenario in his mind, one he had seen over the years since he had this off and on relationship with Gordo. All 300 pounds of Gordo, squeezed into a standard regulation chair, wiping off sweat from his forehead with his usual cloth handkerchief. Behind the sweaty forehead was one of the most brilliant analytical brains that the NSA had ever known. Gordo's rise in the ranks had been spectacular, and for good reason.

"The big man himself. This outbreak has everybody shitting in their pants. It's unchartered waters," Gordo replied.

"POTUS himself?" Kranken said. There was an expectant pause. He took a deep breath. "I need my team. And an unlimited expense account."

"Whomever you want, at whatever price." There was no hesitation. "A private jet is on its way from Miami to pick you up. Should be there in a couple of hours. Get your guys ready. You leave tomorrow night for India from Washington. I'll fill you in when you get to Washington Dulles."

Kranken clicked the line dead. He shut his eyes and took a deep breath. Korea, Africa, the drug busts, bullets whizzing by, the physical injuries, the emotional scars .... all of this buzzed as the mid-sized fishing boat rocked gently. His heart raced, the fists closed tightly to negate the tremor. Kranken threw his head back and opened his eyes slowly. The arms relaxed, and he opened his hands slowly. Rock steady. He looked over at the calm waters. Maybe this was the last big one that he had been hoping for. Grenada was nice and peaceful, but for Kranken, it was losing its sheen. He felt the adrenaline surging. This place was too damn peaceful.

He pulled out his phone and started punching numbers. First, he called Ricky Smits.

"Wallop Sierra?" Kranken said. Somehow the undercover names from a mission a decade ago stuck. "This is Tango Mike."

"Hey, Chief," an obviously surprised voice answered. "What gives?"

"You up for an overseas trip?"

"Overseas?" Ricky's voice was attentive now.

"India—"

"It's that plague thing, isn't it?" Ricky interrupted.

"It's not the plague. But yes, that's where we would be headed."

"Jeeesus…" Ricky's voice tapered. "I thought the previous two jobs were our last jobs."

"I know," Kranken said. "This one would really be the last. Free hand and big money this time because of national security issues."

"Are we officially involved?" This time there was surprise in Ricky's voice. He knew Kranken abhorred rules, protocols, and procedures.

"Yes and no. I'm calling Jigga Lima next. Are you in?" Impatience reflected in Kranken's tone.

Silence spun in for a few seconds.

"I'm in. When do we leave?"

"Get to Washington by tomorrow afternoon and call me. We leave tomorrow night," Kranken said.

"Tomorrow? Goddamit Joe—"

Kranken smiled as he hung up. He then punched in Monty Pugs' number.

"Jigga Lima, Tango Mike here," Kranken said.

"Who? What?" Heavy breathing filtered down the line. "What's happening, Chief?"

"You working out?" Kranken asked. He heard a faint female moan in the background. "Ah...that kind of exercise."

"Yeah, Tango, that kind. This better be important, Boss."

"Overseas trip, lot of flexibility and money. National security issue." Kranken was concise and crisp.

"Overseas where?" Monty asked. His breathing was on even keel now.

"India—"

"It's that plague thing, isn't it?"

Kranken sighed. "It's not the plague. And Sierra's in. You?"

"Hmmm, the usual suspects. I'm in. When and where?" Monty asked.

"Be in Washington by tomorrow afternoon and call me. We leave tomorrow night." Kranken hung up before there was a response. He had worked with these two on numerous occasions in the past. They understood one another completely.

Next afternoon, Joe was in Gordo's office.

"Thanks, Joe," Gordo said. "I owe you one for this."

"Your office hasn't changed in the last decade, Gordo, and neither have you," Joe replied, looking around at the familiar dingy room, in a dingy building, in suburban northern Virginia. The dusty black filing cabinet, tucked in one corner of the room, looked strikingly familiar from a few years ago. Then his eyes settled back on Gordo, who probably still weighed not an ounce less than 300 pounds, distributed disproportionately on a 5 foot 10 inch frame. And, like always, he was sweating profusely.

"Well, you are probably right," Gordo said, wiping his face with his cloth handkerchief. "But the world is changing around us. It's a pessimistic place now."

"Yeah. It's getting complicated," Joe replied.

"You look good, though. Your team in?"

"Thanks. And yes, both are here in DC. What's the latest?"

"As you requested, ten million dollars is in—"

"I meant the latest in India. Any leads?" Kranken said.

"No. It's infinitely worse than whatever you can imagine. The disease, I mean. The details are sketchy. Lot of smoke and rumors. That's what you sort out when you get there. POTUS is very nervous and has every reason to be."

"Do I have support staff there?"

"The Indian Army is in control of the site. And those guys are good. There is a Colonel Biswas, an Infectious Disease specialist, in charge of the medical team. You will have full co-operation from the authorities. James Kichner is our embassy Charge d'affair. All his resources will be at your disposal. And one more thing," Gordo paused to catch his breath.

Kranken waited.

"Dr. John Eters is the CDC team leader on the site," Gordo continued. "I don't know much about him, other than he will cooperate fully. You will have a satellite phone. Keep me updated. Good luck, Joe. Godspeed."

CHAPTER 13

DRIVING BACK TO HIS TOWNHOUSE, JOHN WAS engulfed in a flurry of nostalgia. A mix of anticipation and apprehension seesawed with his emotions. He was not looking forward to the long flight, but he was thinking beyond that. His professional interest was aroused by the severe outbreak, but there was one pestering question that he kept asking himself. Should he contact Rupani? And the answer was always a resounding 'yes'. He did not know if he would be successful. And then again, what would come out of the meeting, if it did happen. He shook his head, and a faint smile touched his lips.

"Got to settle down, man. Calm down. She's probably married with kids by now," he murmured to himself.

He threw some clothes and toiletries in a duffel bag. He then made a beeline for the storage area in his basement. Memories flooded as he rummaged through documents, papers, and old pictures. His eyes searched for a little black diary that held contact info on people from his residency days. There were no smartphones back then. He found the diary and started flipping through the pages as he looked for Rupani's number. A picture fell onto the concrete floor. It was Rupani with Mickey Mouse in the background, during a trip they took in the final year of her ID fellowship. He let out a deep sigh as he thought of that trip and their time together. He took a long look at the picture and then stuck it in his wallet.

John got back to headquarters a few minutes before four. Rupani was alive in his mind now. He recalled how she talked, walked, ate. Everything. In the last hour, he realized he wanted her back. A small voice cautioned him. It had been a long time, and a lot happens in a few years. Was she married? Was she in a steady relationship? But his mind would not go down that path. At this time, there was only anticipation to get there, and then find her. He went straight to Room 2000 and found it to be a busy place. A lot of people milling around, but each, it seemed, with a sense of purpose. Dr. Roberts seemed to be the person in charge. He waved John towards a table with a stern-looking woman in a crisp uniform.

"Hello, your passport please," she said with a smile, transforming the stern face into middle-aged matronly efficiency.

"Hi," John replied and handed her his passport. He looked at her name tag. She was from the State Department.

A line formed behind John.

She flipped through his passport, then looked up at him to match his face with the passport picture. She entered some data in her laptop, and seemed satisfied with the response. She stamped a diplomatic visa.

"You are all done and ready to go," she said, and handed the passport back to him.

"That's it?" John arched his eyebrows.

"That's it, Dr. Eters," she said, with a practiced smile.

"I thought there would be an interview with Indian Embassy officials," said John.

"The Indian government can't get you there fast enough, Doctor. This is a serious international crisis, and the Indian government is being extremely cooperative."

"Well, thank you," John said.

He then walked over to Dr. Roberts' table. He was giving out instructions to a group standing around him. The group dispersed, and he waved John towards him.

"Hi, John," he said, and continued in the same breath. "You will be the Field Team Leader. The entire team will report to you. There will be about one hundred individuals traveling with you on the private plane. About half of them are medical or para-medical personnel. The rest are support staff, communications, security, et cetera."

"We are going by a private charter plane?" John asked, stopping in midstride.

"Yes, courtesy Xenon Pharmaceuticals. They have a number of huge factories in India. One of them is very close to the hot zone. Anyway, here's some more info we received. You can go through this en route. It's a long flight," Dr. Roberts said, handing him a thick file.

"Where do we go after we land in New Delhi?"

"You will be in New Delhi for the first day. You will be briefed and brought up to speed on the situation. The local administration will be extremely helpful. The Indian Army has set up camp about five miles from the outer perimeter of the hot zone. Whatever you need there, just ask James Kichner. He is our Charge d'affair at our embassy in New Delhi. He will be your liaison in India. If whatever you want is doable, he will get it done," Dr. Roberts explained.

John nodded as he took in the information.

"How long do we stay there?" he asked.

"Target time is two weeks. You will have enough time to evaluate the site, get cultures, and compute data. But the return is open ended, so if you need more time, that's fine. Any questions?"

"No. I think I'm okay. I just hope we have enough ground support," John murmured.

"You will have all the help you need. The team will be provided with global satellite phones, so you can call me anytime from any place. The plane will refuel at Ramstein Air Base in Germany for about five hours. You know most of the people in your team already. Good luck." Dr. Roberts stood up and held out his hand.

John shook it with a firm resolve. "I'll keep in touch," he said.

"You do that," Dr. Roberts said. He pulled on John's arm and led him to the side for a quiet word. "This is for your ears only. I got a call from the White House a few minutes ago."

John's eyebrows arched. "The White House?"

Dr. Roberts nodded in the affirmative. "Chief of Staff. A gentleman will meet up with you in Germany. Give him whatever info he asks for, do not ask him too many questions. He is to be given full access to all facilities, labs, documents. Whatever he wants. Don't hold back anything from him—"

"Who is this guy?" John interrupted him. "CIA? NSA?"

"He didn't say, and I didn't ask. And you don't have to either. He has the blessings of the big man himself."

"The President himself?" John said. "What's his name?"

"His name," Dr. Roberts replied, "is Joe Kranken."

"Joe Kranken," John repeated. "I'll remember that."

CHAPTER 14

THE FLIGHT WAS LONG. JOHN WENT THROUGH THE information Dr. Roberts had handed over to him prior to the flight. Richard Kostovo sat with him on the way to Germany. The lavishly equipped 747 was impressive. He stood up to stretch his legs and did a quick survey of the people around him. He saw a lot of familiar faces, mostly from his field team. Some of them waved back at him. He felt comfortable working with people he already knew. They were familiar with his modus operandi. He settled back in his spacious seat as the overhead microphones crackled.

"Ladies and gentlemen, this is Captain Schuser. We will be landing at Ramstein Air Base in about thirty minutes. The local time is 6:10 a.m. and the temperature is a brisk 45 degrees Fahrenheit, with clear skies. We will take off at exactly 12:30 p.m. for New Delhi. Hope you all had a pleasant flight."

"I could get used to riding this baby," Richard remarked.

"Yeah. Maybe you should get a job with Xenon Pharmaceuticals," John replied, his lips curling into a smile.

"So, what words of wisdom are we going to hear from you after we land in Germany?" Richard asked.

"Just logistics and stats," John smiled. "Words of wisdom will come after we solve this sucker."

"Well, if anybody can do it, it's you," Richard replied.

John squared his jaw. Both men realized the importance of this mission.

The plane landed a few minutes later. The airport was more pleasant and welcoming than one would imagine of a military base. But the stark gray walls, bare essential furnishings, and the stoic men and women in uniform left no doubt as to where you were. A memo went around indicating the time and location of the field team meeting.

"We have an hour before the meeting. Let's grab a bite," John said, looking at Rich.

Rich nodded and they followed signs to the cafeteria.

The space designated for the meeting was huge and dwarfed the 100 people gathered there. John surveyed his field team, sitting on metal chairs, facing him. He knew most of them from prior trips. He was one of the five physicians on the entire team. There were microbiologists, lab techs, statisticians, paramedical staff, isolation experts—all specialists in their respective fields.

"I am John Eters. Most of you know me," he started. "We are embarking on a very important mission." He had everyone's attention. "All of you know what's going on in India. We are going in to isolate and identify the pathogen. Once we enter the hot zone, we will collect blood and tissue samples. I want you all to follow protocols to the letter. These protocols are lifesavers in situations precisely like these. If there is anything amiss, even a hint of deviation from protocol procedures, I want that person to withdraw and detox immediately and stay in isolation till the problem is rectified. We all will be working in pairs or threes, so that nobody is ever alone inside the perimeter of the hot zone." He paused.

He spoke clearly and succinctly.

"I don't need to tell you how important it is for us to succeed," he continued. "If this goddamn thing spreads, it means disaster for the entire world. We hope to wrap up our investigative work in two weeks. At whatever point we leave off in India, we will continue from the same point back home." He paused again. He cleared his throat and continued. "As soon as we land in India, we will have a detailed meeting regarding procedures and protocols. The team members will be in constant touch with each other while inside the hot zone. If you notice anything unusual, talk to me. Ask questions, no matter how trivial. There are no dumb questions, only dumb answers."

John then went over routine protocols. The questions were few, as most people there knew what role they had to play. The meeting concluded in an hour.

As John was gathering his papers, a tall, well-built, white man approached him.

"Hi, I am Bill Mckay, Biohazard Security. May I talk to you for a couple of minutes?" he asked, extending his hand.

"McKay?" John said. This wasn't the person Dr. Roberts had mentioned.

"You were expecting somebody else?" McKay asked.

"No…no. I was not expecting anybody. Biohazard security?" John asked, taking McKay's hand. The grip was tight, almost vice-like. "I didn't realize you guys would be here. Dr. Roberts did not mention anything."

"I am not with the CDC. We are an extension of the bioterror prevention wing of the NSA. We will take care of the transportation of samples and cultures from the hot zone. I am sure you realize what could happen if this bug fell into the wrong hands, Doctor."

"How do you plan to transport the specimens and culture plates?" John asked, his brow furrowed. Something did not gel here.

"You just hand over the specimens, tubes, and culture plates to us. We will transport them in an environmentally controlled safe box. It's my problem then."

"I have to check with my superiors, Mr. McKay."

"Of course. You do that. I'll keep in touch. And please call me Bill."

"How many of you are there, Bill?" John asked.

"There's plenty of us spread all around. Please keep this conversation to yourself. No need to cause unnecessary anxiety. I'll see you around, Doc," McKay said, as he walked away.

John nodded without saying a word. His eyebrows were arched as he watched McKay walk away.

"I am going to check you out, Mr. McKay," he said, almost murmuring to himself.

"A good thought, Dr. Eters. But leave that to me," a voice said, right behind him, making him jump.

He turned around to see a man standing right behind him. Where in the hell had he come from?

"Hello, I am Joe Kranken," the man continued, and his lips tilted into a hint of a smile.

"Hi," John said hurriedly, now embarrassed by his own startled reaction. "I didn't hear you."

"Don't worry about McKay. You focus on your job, leave the rest to me," Kranken said.

"Dr. Roberts mentioned you, Mr. Kranken," John said.

"Please call me Joe. Anything new so far, Dr. Eters?"

"And I'm John. No, nothing to add so far," John replied. His eyes swept over Kranken. Probably in his mid-fifties, closely cropped jet-black hair with a hint of silver, about 5-11, wearing black jeans and a light grey shirt, under which taut muscles rippled. A ruggedly handsome face, high cheekbones. John looked at the eyes. He felt a chill run down his spine, as the ice cold, slate gray eyes stared back at him.

"Don't deviate from your protocol, John," Kranken said. "Your own words during your meeting. Don't give McKay anything unless I tell you."

It was not a request. It was certainly not a suggestion. It was an order, without sounding like one.

"Okay, Joe. I'll keep you posted," John said.

"Well, I'll see you in New Delhi," Kranken said.

John watched him walk away. Kranken's walk reminded him of a leopard he had seen on National Geographic videos—quiet, graceful, and lethal.

John dozed off during the flight. He was in that half-asleep, half-awake zone, aided by the steady drone of the engines. Images of the disease's ravaging effects on its victims floated in and out of his subconscious haze. In the shadows behind the pictures, his mind conjured up a silhouette that troubled him. The shadowy figure flitted from one disturbing picture to another. The more his half-asleep brain tried to identify the figure, the more elusive it became. And then suddenly a bright light shone, revealing the side profile of the shadow…Rupani!

John woke up with a start, as the plane went through a turbulent patch.

"Focus, John, focus," he murmured to himself. But despite his efforts, memories flooded his mind.

CHAPTER 15

THE LANDING AT INDIRA GANDHI INTERNATIONAL
Airport, New Delhi, was uneventful. The typical conversation
buzz was noticeably missing. Instead, somber faces were the rule.
A smile was hard to come by. The team was hustled into a large
room, after a long walk through the airport.

"This airport is something, isn't it?" a bleary-eyed Richard said.

"It sure is," John said, staring at the complex motifs, sculp-
tures, and artwork depicting ancient Indian culture.

"I thought it was supposed to be hot and humid here. Seems
pretty good so far."

"We haven't stepped outside the airport yet. It's supposed to
be in the upper nineties with eighty percent humidity," John said.

The formality of paperwork was dealt with quickly. The
Indian officials barely looked at the passports. The escort team
seemed to be in a rush to get the Americans working on this
national calamity.

The team was then herded into an isolated section of the arrival lounge. Refreshments, snacks, fruit juice, and bottled water were stacked neatly on small tables all around the room.

There were a number of uniformed personnel in attendance. An entourage walked in through the main door. Somebody from that team pointed towards John, and a uniformed officer approached him.

"Hi, I am Colonel Biswas, from the Indian Army Research Center. I am the lead investigator for the local team. Welcome, and thanks for coming," he said to John, in a strong, clipped accent.

John took his hand and eyed his crisp, olive green Army uniform. "I am John Eters." The handshake was firm. Colonel Biswas was about six feet tall, well-built, with swarthy dark skin, probably in his mid-forties.

"Any updates? Do we have the index case identified?" John continued.

"I think we might have," Biswas answered. "A ninety-two-year-old gentleman, initials HPS. I'll fill you in with the details on the flight."

"Flight?" John asked.

"To Chandigarh, where we have our command center. It's about thirty kilometers from the hot zone."

"How long is the flight from here to Chandi….?" John asked.

"Chandigarh. The flight from here is about an hour. We will all head to the military airport. Our aircraft is ready."

He spoke precise British English.

Colonel Biswas was all business, and everybody headed towards the exit doors.

The heat and humidity hit everyone like a physical blow as soon as they stepped out to get to the transport buses. The air was heavy and oppressive. Sweating was instantaneous, with clothes sticking to the skin.

John looked around for Kranken. He did not see him. It was a short walk of about 100 yards to the buses.

"You were right," Richard said, walking beside John. "This is suffocating."

"And it's 3 a.m.," John said. "It'll be worse when the sun is out."

"This is going to be a lot of fun," Richard murmured under his breath.

The buses were air conditioned and comfortable. The ride to the military airport was about 30 minutes. Traffic was sparse, and a foggy haze enveloped the entire route. Streetlights bathed the roadways in a surreal, pale-yellow glow. Security vehicles flanked the buses along the route, throwing streaks of red into the mix from the flashing lights.

The three transport buses parked next to a huge military transport aircraft. Two extremely tall, uniformed men, one with a bright red turban and a beard, supporting a bold MP armband on the right upper arms stood on each side of the steps leading up to the aircraft. They were armed with automatic weapons and stood ramrod still.

It was one of those typical humungous planes, with bare essentials inside. The décor was all green, including the seatbelts.

There were rows of four seats on each side, with a narrow aisle in between. The uniformed pilot stood at the top of the steps

"Please start seating from the rear. It's a very short flight," he repeated, in perfect British English.

John, Richard, and Colonel Biswas were the last ones to board the plane. They found seats next to each other at the front of the plane.

"What's the latest, Colonel? Fill me in," John said. He had to speak loudly as the aircraft's engines revved up.

"Nothing good. One hundred more dead or dying. It has spread to the neighboring villages. Total death toll is now about five hundred, in about a week. We have not been able to grow anything in cultures. There are some upper respiratory symptoms initially. The spread may be airborne." Colonel Biswas ran his hand through the short crewcut hair on his head. He shook his head slowly. The plane was now picking up speed on the runway.

"I know it's tough, Colonel," John said.

"It is, Dr. Eters. There are about three to five percent survivors." The colonel's voice was a bit off key, as if he still didn't believe the high percentage of fatalities.

"The survivors have mild URI symptoms for one to two days…and then?" John persisted.

"Then they are just fine. That gives me hope," Colonel Biswas replied. "That implies their B cells have an immediate response to this infection."

"And so?" John knew the colonel's response before he said it.

"And so we are in the process of cloning genes from plasma cells through Next Generation Sequencing and then the CHO cells…." Colonel Biswas paused.

"Chinese Hamster Ovary cells, the factories for producing antibodies." John permitted himself a smile.

"That's where we need your help, John," Colonel Biswas said.

"You need the fermenters to purify and mass produce the antibodies," John said, his mind in hyperdrive.

"Yes, we do," Colonel Biswas said.

The fermenters in question are almost two-story high structures of sophisticated biotech equipment, used to purify mass-produced antibodies from the supernatant fluid.

"Done," John replied. "We can have the samples flown out as soon as you can get them to me and I'll have the CDC on it. We should have the serum back in less than a week."

"Thank you," Colonel Biswas said, his voice awash in relief. "Let's get this going as soon as we reach Chandigarh."

"Let's hope we can solve this together. We can't afford to let this spread," John said.

The shuddering and shaking of their seats ceased as the plane left the tarmac.

Colonel Biswas nodded. "It is brave and kind of you to come here. We are in your debt."

"Nothing like that, Colonel. The whole world is in this together. If this gets out, we are all in trouble. Were you able to identify the index case?"

"Yes. We are almost certain. The first person to die. Hari Prasad Sharma or HPS. Started with a fever, cough followed by rash, and then the hemorrhagic cutaneous manifestations. He was in the hospital for four days before he died. He was ninety-two."

"Ninety-two?"

"Yes, and the total course of the illness in him and younger patients was about the same. From the onset of symptoms till death…about one to two weeks."

"Doctors, nurses in the hospital who were looking after him?" John was wide awake now, his inherent medical curiosity aroused.

"Most of them have the infection. I think three out of fifteen are okay. Everyone else is very ill. Some are already dead." Colonel Biswas held onto the armrest as the plane hit a mild turbulent patch. "All contacts are being quarantined now."

John scratched his head.

"How about HPS's family members? Can we talk to them?" he asked Colonel Biswas.

"He lived with his son, daughter-in-law, and granddaughter— all dead. A grandson is in the United States."

"In the States? Do we know where?" John asked.

"We were hoping you would help us locate him, with all your resources. We just have his name so far. It's important to talk to him. He was probably talking to his family when they were sick. He might have some crucial information," Colonel Biswas said.

"Give me his name, and we will get our people on it."

"Arthik Sharma, in his late twenties. He is probably in the Washington, DC, area."

"We will find him," John said. "We should have this guy localized in a day or so. Tell me more about this illness. What's your gut feeling?"

Colonel Biswas rubbed his cheek and stared intently into space.

A metallic voice came over the PA system. "We are starting our descent and will be landing in Chandigarh in ten minutes."

Colonel Biswas thought for a long moment. "It's nothing like any virus that medical science knows about so far. The contagious phase seems to be during incubation and early stages. It's not contagious after the rash starts fulminating and bleeding."

John thought about it for a moment. "This virus—whatever this goddamn thing is—finishes its life cycle before it kills the host."

"Seems like that. It's deadly, with about ninety-five percent mortality. We still don't know the carrier—is it an animal host?"

Now it was John's turn to be lost in thought. "The contagious phase is when the patient is not very ill. That makes it so much more difficult to contain. There has to be an animal host…" His voice trailed off.

"And we have security issues. The hot zone is not far from the border with Pakistan. The Army has a secure perimeter around the area. If this virus falls into the wrong hands, the results would be disastrous for the entire world," Colonel Biswas said.

The transport plane lumbered onto the military airport in Chandigarh and taxied to a stop.

"You all will be staying at Hotel Mount View. You will have almost the entire hotel to yourself. There are hardly any visitors to this town since this outbreak. People are scared." There was steel in the colonel's voice. "We will get to the base camp in a few hours. You rest up in the meantime."

John nodded. He looked at his phone. 4 a.m.

"I can barely keep my eyes open. Thanks for everything. We will see you in a few hours," John said as he wiped the sweat off his brow. "God, it's humid here."

"That it is," Colonel Biswas smiled. "Get in the bus, it's air conditioned."

The drive to the hotel was through the town of Chandigarh. There was hardly any traffic at this hour. The city looked clean, with tree-lined, wide roads. Shuttered shops had bright neon signs flashing their wares. There were some people milling around a couple of nightclubs, evidenced by brightly lit semi-nude motifs of dancing women.

"Nightlife goes on," Rich remarked, with a smile.

"Life itself goes on. You got to do what you got to do," John said, adding to the smile.

It was about 4:30 a.m. by the time they got to the hotel. The hotel staff was waiting for them. Members of the team were paired, two in each room.

"It's you and me in a room, Rich," John said.

"Okay, Boss, let's hit the pillows," Richard replied.

"Amen to that."

They walked to their room on the second floor. Richard unlocked the door and flipped the lightswitch on.

"Jesus Christ—" Rich exclaimed.

"Welcome, Docs, how was the flight?" Joe Kranken asked. He was sitting on a chair across the room, a slight smile touching his lips. Monty slouched by the window.

John and Rich were wide awake now.

"How…how long have you been waiting for us?" John managed to find his tongue. "And how did you know my room number?"

"Don't worry about minor details. This is Monty Pugs, my associate," Joe said, pointing towards him.

"This is Richard Kostovo, lead microbiologist on the team."

"Pleased to make your acquaintance, Dr. Kostovo. I am Joe Kranken. Now fill me in quick and then you boys rest up."

John threw his bag on the floor and flopped on the sofa. He filled Kranken in with whatever Colonel Biswas had told him. Joe Kranken listened intently, asking a few questions here and there.

"Arthik Sharma. Is that what you said his name was? We've got to find him and see if he has a few pieces of the puzzle. Now you guys rest up. You have a busy few days ahead," Joe said.

"A-R-T-H-I-K. I'll call Dr. Roberts, and he can get in touch with the authorities to find him—"

"Don't worry about Arthik. We will have his location soon. I'll let you know."

Kranken and Monty walked out the door.

"Who is that?" Rich asked.

"I just know the name. Seems to have blessing from the top of the food chain," John said.

"I have a feeling he does not need anyone's blessing. He makes me nervous," Richard said. He shuddered as he remembered the cold, slate grey eyes.

"You too? I thought it was just me," John replied.

CHAPTER 16

ARTHIK STARED AT THE BLACK TRASH BAG, OCCUPY-
ing a corner of his walk-in closet. His father's halting voice
reverberated.

"We are all sick…"

He grabbed a few Ziplock bags and distributed the $100 bills
between his check-in bag, his wallet, and his carry-on. If there was
a problem at the airport in India, he would figure it out there. He
would figure out how to pay Keith back when he returned. Ajeet
would be there in a few minutes. He had offered to drop him off at
the airport, which Arthik had gladly accepted. He was not going
to mention anything about this money to Ajeet.

His doorbell rang in a few minutes.

"Hi, Ajeet, thanks for giving me a ride to the airport," Arthik
said as he opened the door.

"Oh, not at all, Arthik. I just hope all is well when you
get home."

"I hope so, too," Arthik said, and his brow crinkled.

"Do you need me to do anything while you are gone?" Ajeet asked.

"No, thank you, Ajeet. Avtar has the keys to the apartment. He'll keep checking off and on."

In a few minutes, they were on the Dulles Airport access road. Arthik stared straight ahead, his hands clenched.

"Don't worry, Arthik, you are doing all you can do. The rest is in God's hands. Be a real *Punjabi Gabru.*"

Arthik looked at him, and he gave a weak smile.

"I'll try my best, Ajeet. And thank you for everything you have done for me."

"Oh, come on. It's the least I can do for you," Ajeet replied. He paused for a moment. "I hate to ask, but can you do me a favor?"

"Anything, Ajeet. Anything for you," Arthik said.

"Can you take some things to India for me? It's my brother's stuff. He left it here when he visited me last year."

"Oh, sure. There's a lot of room in my bag—"

"I'll just give you a bag that you can check in. My brother will meet you at the airport to get the bag. Is that okay with you?" Ajeet asked.

"Oh, sure, Ajeet. That is not a problem at all," Arthik said. It felt good that he could do something in return for the person who had done so much for him.

Arthik's flight touched down in New Delhi at 1:30 a.m. The plane was half empty. The ambience and sophistication of the Indira

Gandhi International Airport, which had left him awestruck a year ago, was now lost on him. He half-ran, half-walked to the immigration counters.

"The purpose of your visit, sir?" the immigration official asked, the tone stiff as usual.

"I am here to see my family. They are in Majra," Arthik blurted out.

The eyes of the official softened. He paused for a second and then started stamping the passport.

"From Majra itself or surrounding area?" he asked.

"Majra. My grandfather, parents, and sister are still there." Arthik was surprised his voice was steady. His insides were in a turmoil.

"Have you been able to talk to them?" the official asked, his face had a concerned frown.

"No," Arthik replied. He paused for a moment. "I have been trying to call for the last two days, but the calls are not going through."

"From what I have read and heard, nobody survived in that village. I am sorry," the official said, handing him the passport.

Arthik just nodded, not trusting himself to speak. He had heard and read as much. It was headline news everywhere. Maybe his parents and sister were in an on-site hospital or something. He had heard there was a CDC team on its way now. His mind shut out the possibility his family had perished.

He walked up to the baggage claim area and waited for his bags. The baggage belt was moving, and Arthik pushed to the front of the crowd. After a couple of minutes, he saw his bag and pulled it off the belt. He squinted along the entire length of the belt, snaking around a wide area. He could not see Ajeet's bag. He looked at his watch. 2:15 a.m. He walked around the belt, hoping to catch a glimpse of the bag. Passing minutes seemed like hours. He waited a little while longer.

2:45 a.m.

He pulled out his phone and dialed Ajeet's number.

"Hello, Ajeet, this is Arthik."

"Hi, Arthik. You are in New Delhi?" Ajeet's voice crackled in his ear.

"Landed about an hour and a half ago. I've been waiting at baggage claim for more than forty-five minutes now. Your bag has not shown up. What should I do?"

There was a short pause.

"Don't worry about my bag, Arthik. I'll call my brother. I know you are anxious to get to your family. You go ahead, and good luck," Ajeet said.

"What about your bag?" Arthik asked.

"It's okay, Arthik. My brother has connections at the airport. He'll work something out. You get home and keep in touch." The line clicked dead.

Arthik walked through the green channel. Nobody asked him to open his bags. He then went to the Thomas Cook money exchange booth and converted $5,000 from one of the Ziplock bags to Indian rupees. As he stepped out of the enclosed area, into the muggy Delhi night, the heat and humidity hit him in an instant. The air hung heavy, but Arthik was oblivious. He hailed a taxi.

"Where to, sahib?" the driver asked.

"Majra, near Chandigarh," Arthik said, and waited for the expected response.

The cab driver's eyes opened wide. "Are you serious?" he asked.

"Yes," Arthik replied. He had expected this response. He waited for more.

"People are dying there, sahib," the cabbie said, shaking his head. "It's like the demons attacked. Nobody lived to tell what happened. People say the next place to get hit will be Chandigarh. Nobody will take you there."

Arthik was prepared. He brandished a wad of Indian rupees that he had exchanged inside the terminal.

"This is twenty thousand rupees. You get another twenty when we get to Chandigarh. Deal?" he asked.

The cabbie's eyes were locked on the money. That was four times the normal fare. He nodded slowly.

"I'll take you to Kharar. Not into the town. Okay with you, sahib?"

Arthik nodded. Kharar was a small town on the outskirts of Chandigarh.

"That's fine. And don't call me sahib. Name's Arthik." He threw his duffel bag on the backseat and got in the front passenger seat.

"Okay, Arthik ji. I am Rajan."

It took them an hour to get out of Delhi.

"Why do you want to go there?" Rajan asked.

"My family's there. In Majra."

Rajan shook his head and looked at him. "Nobody survived there," he said quietly.

Arthik just stared ahead at the road. His mind was trying to wrap around the fact that he might not see his family ever again. Every time his brain started to go there, he felt his throat tighten and his heart pump so hard, it seemed his ears would blow out. He took a few quick long breaths.

"It's okay, Arthik ji," Rajan said. "Maybe they are in a hospital. I know the Army is taking care of everybody there."

Arthik nodded. He didn't want to say anything. He knew his voice would tremble. He looked out the window at the rapidly moving landscape. Traffic was thin now and got thinner as they moved away from Delhi.

"We are nearing Ambala. You heard about *Kake da Dhaba*?" Rajan asked. He was referring to a roadside, open-air eating place along National Highway 1, three hours north of New Delhi. Over the years, this roadside eating joint had earned almost an iconic status. *Dhabas* are roadside cafes, peppered along major highways, especially in northern India.

Arthik looked at him and permitted himself a slight smile.

"You are hungry," Arthik said. "I went to the US just a year ago. I've been to *Kake da Dhaba* a number of times."

Rajan pulled off the road, and Arthik recognized the place instantly. String lights ran from one 20-foot pole to another, over haphazardly placed tables, under the stars. The place was busy, but not as busy as Arthik remembered from three to four years ago.

Rajan waved him to a table near the open-air kitchen. There were three cooks working at a time and sat about five feet high on a brick ledge, which had tandoors (brick ovens), used to bake fresh bread. There were about five gas grills with pots of varying sizes on them. The fragrance of spices and condiments intermingled with marinated meat and vegetables wafted through the open air. Arthik's stomach growled.

"That was a good break," Arthik said, as Rajan pulled away to the main road.

"You were hungry, too," Rajan said.

"Yes, I was." Arthik put his head back and shut his eyes for a moment.

"Go to sleep, Arthik ji. I will wake you up when we get to Kharar. It's still three hours away."

Arthik woke to the gentle prodding by Rajan.

"We are at Kharar," Rajan said.

Arthik rubbed his eyes and looked at his watch. 9 a.m. Rajan had parked in front of a gas station. Plenty of people milled around. Inquisitive kids peeked into the car. Arthik got out of the car and stretched.

"You got some rest, Arthik ji," Rajan said. "Do you have a place to stay here in town?"

"No, I don't. I'm not staying here anyway. I have to get to Chandigarh," Arthik replied.

"It's going to be tough. No public transportation is going into town. People are scared. There's an occasional private car on the road, but a lot of Army trucks," Rajan said, and he pointed to a convoy of green Army trucks parked a few hundred yards ahead.

"Thank you, Rajan," Arthik said, and handed him the promised money. "I think I'm going to talk to the soldiers and see if they'll give me a ride."

Arthik threw his duffel bag on his shoulder, grabbed his bag, and walked briskly towards the Army trucks.

"Fill out your name, address, and cell phone number on this form. We leave in fifteen minutes," the lieutenant said. He had been very sympathetic to Arthik's earnest efforts to get to his family.

"Thank you, Lieutenant," Arthik said, a weight lifted off his shoulders. "I appreciate this very much."

"You are welcome, Arthik. I hope you find your family."

In 15 minutes, the convoy was on the move. Arthik rode in the back of one of the trucks. The soldiers sitting beside him were not talkative, all sitting ramrod straight, with automatic rifles between their knees.

The ride was bumpy. As the trucks sped towards Chandigarh, Arthik noticed that the traffic was light, a very unusual feature on a weekday morning. Green fields, growing maize and rice whisked by. Cattle grazed lazily, and children interrupted their ramshackle, dusty roadside cricket games to give curious looks to the convoy of green trucks speeding along.

Chandigarh was no different. Traffic was sparse. Stray dogs roamed in packs, some of them exploring overturned trashcans. He did not see many people. Soldiers moved about in twos and threes. The convoy rumbled to a stop.

A familiar face came around looking for Arthik.

"Hey, Arthik, where do you want to go?" Lieutenant Anand asked.

"Anywhere is fine. I am going to look for a hotel room," Arthik replied.

The lieutenant shook his head. "The only hotel open is Mount View, because it is run by the government. We are going to pass about a block from there. You can get off there."

"Thanks, Lieutenant. I really appreciate it."

"You are welcome. Good luck."

Arthik walked the one block distance after being dropped off. His shirt was drenched with sweat by the time he reached the hotel. He walked up the brick paved driveway to the double door entrance. The famous manicured gardens of Hotel Mount View showed signs of wear and tear, probably due to the lack of manpower. SUVs and Army trucks were parked along the entire length of the driveway. He walked into the lobby, and the chill of the air conditioning enveloped him like a blessing. There was nobody at the reception desk. He rang the bell on the counter and waited. He looked around at the bare lobby.

"How can I help you, Sir?" a voice said from behind the counter.

THE ECHO OF FOOTPRINTS

Arthik turned around and looked at a short, elderly, turbaned man. A thick, white beard covered most of his face. He wore a crinkly smile.

"Namaste. I need a room," Arthik said in Hindi, and returned the favor of a smile.

The bearded man paused. He looked at him closely for a minute and then his eyes lit up.

"Ah, you must be a part of the American team. Are you a doctor?" he asked.

"No. American team? What American team?" Arthik said, his eyebrows arched. His ever present fatigue left him for the moment.

"You are not with the Americans? They are here to help us with this tragedy. They are all staying here at this Hotel. Why are you here then, son? Almost everyone who can leave, has left Chandigarh."

Arthik hung his head for a moment. "I know. My family was in Majra. I am here to look for them."

The bearded man shook his head slowly. "I'm sorry, son. From what I've heard, nobody survived in that village. My name is Balbir. I am sorry," he repeated himself.

"They might have got out," Arthik's voice trailed off. His heart pounded, and a familiar sinking sensation ensued.

"They might have. Where have you come from?" Balbir asked.

"From America. My name is Arthik Sharma. Tell me about the Americans here. When did they arrive?"

"Early this morning. They are here to help us kill this disease. God bless them," Balbir said. He turned around and grabbed a pair of keys hanging on the wall. "Room 202."

"Thank you, Balbir ji. How can I get to Majra?"

"You can't. Nobody is allowed there since this disease hit. All roads are blocked off by the Army," Balbir said.

"I have to go there. I have to look for my family," Arthik said, a hint of desperation creeping into his voice.

"There is no one left in that village. Maybe you can ask one of the Indian Army officers. They are all around town," Balbir said, as he looked at the elevator door open at the far end of the lobby. "There's some of the Americans."

Arthik followed his gaze and saw a group of people step out of the elevator, in bright yellow T-shirts, with CDC emblazoned across the chest.

"Thanks, Balbir ji," Arthik said, as he walked towards them. "Maybe these guys can help me," he murmured under his breath.

CHAPTER 17

KRANKEN EYED THE VAST ARRAY OF LAPTOP SCREENS spread across three tables in their room.

"You all set up?" he asked Monty, who was busy typing away on a keyboard, flashing multiple, tiny lights.

"I am all set up. We are ready to roll, Chief," Monty replied, his fingers doing a dance on the keyboard.

"Then find me Arthik Sharma," Kranken said.

"Already working on it. There are 253 people with the same name in the United States, twenty that match his age. There is one in Sterling, Virginia, which is about thirty miles west of DC."

"Sterling? That's our guy," Kranken said.

"I thought so. I have his social, address, and copies of his payroll stubs," Monty said, almost speaking to himself.

"You did all this in this past hour?" Kranken asked, cocking an eyebrow.

"Any teenager can do this, Chief," Monty said. "And if you give me a second…bingo! We have his picture," he said rubbing his hands. He punched a keyboard, and Arthik's picture appeared on all three screens.

Kranken stepped closer. "That's his driver's license." He was speechless.

"Yes, Chief. One of the easiest hacks is the DMV. Good-looking guy, this Arthik. Give me another thirty minutes, and I will give you his credit card purchases, his rent…everything."

Kranken was familiar with the gleam in Monty's eyes. He knew Monty would have whatever was available on the web for Arthik Sharma in little time.

"I'll step out and let you work. Where's Ricky?" Kranken asked.

"He just went to check things out."

Kranken nodded in approval and stepped out into the hall-way. He loved working with these two. In the next couple of hours, Ricky would have the lay of the land, as he liked to call it. He would have details of the hotel, exits, transportation, staff, and surroundings, among other things. Logistics was not an issue with Ricky around. And on top of everything else, Ricky was a sharp-shooter from his Navy Seal days. That skill had helped Kranken more than once in the past. As he walked to the lobby, he noticed a familiar face. Bill McKay, the shady biohazard security specialist, was talking animatedly on the phone. He had his hand cupped around his mouth. Kranken stepped back in the shadows and pulled out his phone. He dialed Ricky's number.

"What's up, Chief?" Ricky's voice answered.

"I need you to keep tabs on a Bill McKay. Right now he is in the hotel lobby. He is about six feet, well-built, blue jeans, and light green T-shirt."

"The biohazard security specialist?"

"That's what he calls himself," Kranken replied.

"I'll be there in fifteen."

"Let me know when you have eyes on him. And Ricky?" Kranken waited patiently.

"Yes, Chief?"

"No interaction. No intervention. Just observe. Got it?"

"Got it." The line clicked dead.

He then dialed Gordo's number.

"Yeah?" a sleepy voice answered.

"What do you know about biohazard security team on our flight?" Kranken asked.

"What? Biohazard team?" Gordo was not awake yet.

"Wake up, Gordo. You know anything about a biohazard security team?" Kranken repeated.

There was heavy panting and grunting on the other end.

"I am not aware of any such team on the flight. I'll look into it," Gordo said, sounding awake now.

"Do you know a Bill McKay? Says he is with biohazard security, and wants to have access to the bug, whenever that is isolated."

There was a short silence.

"Make sure that does not happen. I don't know who this guy is, but I'll have him checked out. Watch him." Gordo was more than awake now.

Monty could not believe it.

"Holy crap!" he let out. He dialed Kranken's number.

"Yeah, Monty. What's happening?"

"You close by? I think I found Arthik Sharma," Monty said.

Kranken walked in after a few minutes.

"Okay, Monty, where is he?"

"Closer than you think. Our lad—"

"Lad?"

"Our guy," Monty rolled his eyes, "Arthik Sharma, took a flight to India from Dulles Airport two days ago and reached New Delhi the same night we did. More importantly, about a month ago, he bought an iPhone 5 from the Apple Store in Reston, in northern Virginia."

"You have that phone number?" Kranken asked.

"Yes, I do. I ran a trace on its location." Monty paused and shook his head. "Arthik Sharma is in this hotel right now."

"What...?" Kranken stepped towards the computer.

Monty pointed towards a faint blue dot on one of the screens. "That's his phone, and here is my phone tracer." The two almost overlapped.

Kranken whipped out his phone. "Give me his number. You call the good doctor and tell him that we will have Arthik Sharma in his room in the next ten minutes."

Kranken then dialed Arthik's number.

"Hello?" A hesitant voice answered.

"Mr. Arthik Sharma?" Kranken asked.

"Yes?"

"Mr. Sharma, my name is Joe Kranken. I am with the CDC team. I need to see you," Kranken said.

"You need to see me? Why? I am in India right now," Arthik said, his voice laced with confusion.

"I'm sorry. I should have told you. I am also in Hotel Mount View, in Chandigarh," Kranken explained.

There was a short pause.

"How do you know I am here?" There was a little apprehension in Arthik's voice now.

"It's a long story, Mr. Sharma. Can we meet in the hotel lobby in the next five minutes? I'll explain everything."

"Yeah…sure."

Kranken watched a tall, strong, lithe young man walk into the lobby. He recognized him from the picture. He walked towards Arthik.

"Hi, I'm Joe Kranken," he said, extending his hand.

Arthik took his hand in a strong grip.

"Hi," Arthik replied. "What is going on, Mr. Kranken?"

"Please call me Joe, Arthik," he replied. "I am here with the US contingent to contain this outbreak. There are a few people who want to talk to you because you are from this village. Let's go to my room. I'll explain as we walk."

CHAPTER 18

ARTHIK LOOKED AROUND THE ROOM.

"How was your flight, Mr. Sharma?" John asked, after introductions had been made.

"It was okay. Please call me Art," Arthik replied. "Why am I here? Am I in trouble or something?"

"Nothing like that. As I mentioned before to you, Dr. Eters wants to talk to you, in relation to this epidemic here. He represents the CDC," Kranken said, pointing towards John.

"Why did you want to talk to me?" Arthik asked, his tone hesitant. He looked at John. He was relieved to look away from Kranken, whose eyes made him nervous.

"Please sit down, Arthik," John said, pointing to an empty chair. "I suppose you traveled all the way here to enquire about your family?"

"Yes. I know my grandfather died, but I have not been able to get in touch with my parents and my sister."

There was a long, two-second silence. Then John cleared his throat.

"Art, please call me John. I have bad news for you. From what I have heard from people on the ground here, your family did not survive," John said, and he took a deep breath.

Arthik's stomach clenched as his heart thumped, wanting to burst out of his chest. "Out of all the people who died, how can you be so sure about my family?" he asked, though his tone did not conceal the slightest crack in it.

"Because your grandfather is believed to be the index case of this epidemic. He has been identified as the first case to get this deadly disease." John paused.

It was Arthik's turn now to take a deep breath. He put his head in his hands.

"I'm sorry," John said. His voice was soft.

Kranken and Monty stood by the door. No expressions crossed their faces. Richard Kostovo sat quietly on the bed.

"Are…are you sure?" Arthik asked, looking again at John.

"I got the information directly from Colonel Biswas, the team leader on the ground here."

Arthik looked away, so that nobody would see his eyes moisten.

The room was quiet. Arthik ran his hands through his thick hair.

"So why do you want to talk to me?" he asked, looking at John.

"We are looking for clues. How your grandfather got the disease is the key to finding a cure, or to find a way to prevent further spread of this deadly epidemic. Did you talk to your family when he was sick?"

"Yes. Almost every day," Arthik said.

"I know it's a very tough time for you. But please think back and try to remember everything they told you about him. His symptoms. The first symptoms your parents and sister got. Whatever they told you. One tiny detail, however insignificant, might be the most important one," John said. He paused to let his words sink in. He had the undivided attention of everyone in the room.

Arthik stood up and shook his head, as if to shake the haze off his brain. He started to say something.

John raised his hand. "I know you are tired, Arthik. Go to your room and get some sleep. Whatever you remember, note it down in your smart phone."

"What is done to the bodies of people who died in this epidemic?" Arthik asked.

There was another short, uncomfortable silence.

"After taking samples, biopsies from different organs, the bodies are incinerated," John said. "I am sorry, Arthik."

"I want to go to my village. My house," Arthik said in a steady voice.

The silence was heavy.

"Sorry, you can't. It's still a hot zone—" John started.

"Are you going in there?" Arthik asked.

"Yes."

"Are these guys going in with you?" Arthik asked, waving a hand towards Kranken and Monty.

John nodded affirmative.

Arthik spread out his arms, his palms facing heavenwards. "Then I'm going with you. You have my phone number. Please call me thirty minutes before we leave. Nice meeting all of you."

He nodded and walked out the door.

Kranken permitted himself a smile. "I like that guy."

Arthik woke to the incessant ringing of his phone.

"Hotel lobby. In thirty minutes," a voice said, cutting through the fog of haze in his brain.

"Yeah," Arthik mumbled. He recognized the voice despite being half-asleep. It was that guy Kranken, with the ice-cold eyes. Eyes that gave him the creeps. He dragged himself to the shower.

Arthik let the cold water wash over him, waking him up with a rush of discomfort. He tried to remember his father's phone call when his grandfather had been sick. He tried to concentrate...was it the fever, cough, or the rash that had come first? He wasn't sure. He was going to see his home today. He had an empty, gnawing feeling as images of his family flashed across his mind. He let the tears run, the water washing them down his face.

"You found Arthik Sharma in this hotel?" Colonel Biswas was incredulous.

"I didn't find him, Joe Kranken did," John said.

"That is astounding. Who is he?" the Colonel asked, suitably impressed.

"Part of the security team," John said. "He will be accompanying us to the hot zone today. Ah…here he is." He pointed to Joe Kranken, who was walking down the stairs.

"Hey, Joe, this is Colonel Biswas. He is the field team lead on the ground here." John started the introductions.

"My pleasure, Colonel. This is Monty Pugs," Kranken said, pointing towards Monty, walking behind him.

"I am impressed. Thanks to you and your team for locating Arthik Sharma, Mr. Kranken," Colonel Biswas said.

"Monty has some special skills," Kranken replied.

Colonel Biswas nodded and quickly looked away from Kranken's piercing gaze.

Just then Arthik walked into the lobby.

"This is Art Sharma, Colonel," Kranken said.

"Namaste, Mr. Sharma. I am Colonel Biswas. Please accept my condolences on the passing of your family."

"Thank you, Colonel," Arthik replied.

"Please follow me. The drive to the base camp is about forty-five minutes. We get our protective gear at the camp and from there we will head to Majra."

The ride to the base camp was quiet. It was one of the numerous army SUVs that Arthik had seen on the road from Kharar to Chandigarh. Colonel Biswas sat in the front with the driver. Arthik sat in the middle in the rear, between Kranken and John Eters. Richard Kostovo had stayed behind at the hotel to work on supplies and logistics.

"You slept some?" John asked, looking at Arthik.

"Some," Arthik nodded.

"I am sorry to push this, but I want you to tell me in detail, whatever you remember about the course of your grandfather's illness," John said.

Arthik nodded as he looked out the window at the barren streets. "There was nothing specific. He felt weak, had a fever, cough, and then got the rash in the end. Then my parents got similar symptoms. I think along with a fever."

"Your parents got the rash, cough, and the fever at the same time?" John was persistent, but his tone was soft.

"I think so," Arthik responded.

Just then Kranken's phone buzzed.

"Yes, Ricky?" Kranken said into the phone.

"Hey, Chief, this guy McKay is up to no good. He walked a couple of blocks from the hotel and met up with somebody at a roadside cafe. He is chatting with them right now. I can see him from the window."

"Keep eyes on him as long as you can. Get pictures if possible. Don't blow your cover," Kranken said, as he rubbed his hand on his cheek.

"Already got some pictures, Chief."

"When you get back to the hotel, hook up with Monty and run the pictures through the database. Not a word to anyone. No one." Kranken clicked the line dead. He looked up to see Arthik eyeing him.

"You don't trust many people," Arthik said. It was not a question.

"In my line of work, trust is a luxury I can't afford. Suspicion and mistrust keep me alive," Kranken said, in an even voice. The ice-cold eyes got colder.

There were three checkpoints manned by Army personnel, before they got into the base camp. In spite of Colonel Biswas sitting up front, the soldiers were very thorough. Respectful, polite, but firm.

About 50 yards before the third checkpoint, Arthik suddenly sat up straight. He leaned forward and put his hand on Colonel Biswas' shoulder.

"Stop the car," he said, pointing to an old man sitting on the side of the road.

"Pull up," Colonel Biswas said to the driver. "What is it?" he continued, looking at Arthik.

"I think I know this man from my village," Arthik replied.

The vehicle slowed and came to a stop.

"Your village? Everybody in that village is accounted for, and surviving members are in isolation. This fakir has been here for a few days. His ramblings make no sense. Our jawans give him food every day. He says he has nowhere to go," Colonel Biswas said.

"I need to see him from close up. I want to be sure," Arthik said, stepping out of the SUV.

John and Kranken followed.

The old man looked up as Arthik approached. He was laying down on the side of the road, on a pile of flattened cardboard boxes. He wore a tattered green shirt. His pants were camouflage green, a few sizes too big for his frail frame. His bare feet exposed leathery skin and numerous calluses, thickened by the assault of hot asphalt. An emaciated body peeked through the torn shirt. His hair was matted and dry, stretching to his shoulders. A long-stemmed umbrella protected him from the sun, the stem forced into a pile of dirt. The coarse beard was short, and thin dry lips were pursed as a startlingly clear whistling sound emanated from his mouth. It had a definite rhythm to it, which Arthik recognized. It was an old Hindi song.

"This is *Seeti* baba, from our village," Arthik said, as he knelt beside the old man.

"You sure?" Colonel Biswas asked.

"Yes. He used to wander the streets in our village. He has no family. He would always whistle tunes of old Hindi songs and mumble to himself. His ramblings never made sense. People would give him food and clothes," Arthik said. "*Seeti* means whistle in Hindi," he continued, looking at Kranken.

"He belongs to the five percent that did not get sick?" John asked, looking at Colonel Biswas.

"Probably," Colonel Biswas said.

"If he has not got sick so far, we should run the same tests you are running for other survivors for antibodies."

By that time, Arthik had put his hand behind the old man's neck and propped him up.

"*Seeti* baba," he said loudly in the man's ear.

The whistling ceased, and the crinkly eyes squinted and focused on Arthik's face. *Seeti* baba's hand gently touched Arthik's cheek. The touch barely connected, but it felt as if a thornbush had rubbed against his face.

"Who are you?" *Seeti* baba asked in Hindi, looking at Arthik. His voice was raspy, but strong.

"I am Arthik. I used to live in Majra. How are you, baba?"

"Majra gone. The devil burnt everybody. Everyone is gone." *Seeti* baba's eyes moistened. "But they will be back. I will wait for them here. Will you wait here with me?"

Arthik felt his throat catch. "I will, baba. I will."

"There is nobody in the village. I went there last night—"

"You went in last night?!" The Colonel went on his knee now. "How?"

The baba moved his head imperceptibly towards him for a moment, and then he looked straight at Arthik.

"He doesn't know about the tunnel, does he?" the baba whispered.

"Which tunnel, baba?" Arthik asked.

"The one by the stream, under the temple. You've been there, haven't you?" *Seeti* baba said, his face contorted in a frown.

"The one with snakes?" Arthik's eyebrows were arched.

Seeti baba's face broke into a toothless smile. "Those snakes are my friends. They don't bother me."

"How many times have you been in the village, baba?" Colonel Biswas asked.

"Many, many times. I held my friends when they were dying. The devil took them. I know they will be back. I go there every night and wait for them." The *Seeti* baba settled back on his cardboard bed, and the whistling started again.

"Tell me more about him," John said, looking at Arthik.

"I remember him ever since I was a kid. He used to whistle tunes of Hindi songs. He was the classical crazy old man in the village. A celebrity of sorts. I don't think he ever set a foot outside the village. He has a shack on the north side. Mostly ate whatever people offered him," Arthik said.

"Does that tunnel really exist?" Kranken asked.

"I don't know. I thought it was just a story…a fable. I really don't know." Arthik ran his hands through his hair, now matted with sweat.

"Well, we need to find out," Kranken replied.

"I'll get my men on it," Colonel Biswas said. "In the meantime, we will get him to the hospital and get all the baseline tests and immunology profile done."

The base camp was like a small, bustling, tent city. It was hot and humid, but the breeze made it bearable. John took a deep breath.

"It's a little better than inside the city, isn't it?" Colonel Biswas remarked.

"Barely," John replied, with a hint of a smile.

The colonel took them to a huge hangar-like tent.

"Wow!" John exclaimed, as he took in the cavernous interior.

It was bigger than three football fields put together. There were hundreds of Army uniforms all around. But everything seemed precise, with a purpose. There was no hurrying. Everybody seemed to be doing exactly what they were supposed to. There were rows of desks, and cubicles with hundreds of computer screens flashing.

"Very impressive, Colonel," Kranken remarked.

Colonel Biswas seemed a little taken aback by the appreciation. He shrugged it off.

"Let's get to the scrubbing area. Follow me," he said.

They walked along the entire length of the tent and then through three screen doors with negative air flow into another smaller tent area. This area was much quieter.

"All three of you are going in?" Colonel Biswas asked.

"Yes," John said.

"Okay, then. Dr. Eters knows this stuff, but for the benefit of you two," he pointed towards Arthik and Kranken, "you need to know that you are heading into a hot zone, which means there is a possibility that you could get infected with this goddamned affliction, whatever it is. Please follow instructions for the personal protective gear to the letter. At any time, if you feel your protection has been breached, just stay there and pull the blue string on the front of your suit. That will set off an alarm here and a team will get to you in a few minutes. Please follow instructions of that team leader. You will then be quarantined, though it's hard to say for how long. Any questions?"

There was a short pause.

"We understand, Colonel," Kranken said.

Colonel Biswas waved a hand, and two nurses hurried towards them.

"These two are our best infectious disease nurses. Lieutenant Kavita and Lieutenant Sunanda. They will help you get into your protective gear. If you don't understand any step or procedure, please ask questions. It could be the difference between life and death."

The two nurses smiled and got to work, one with Kranken and the other with Arthik. John and the colonel helped each other. It took 15 minutes to get into the PPG. There were three protective layers, each sealed separately, on top of one another. Then the headgear snapped on.

Arthik looked at the others, and was reminded of pictures of Neil Armstrong landing on the moon. But to his surprise, he was able to move easier than he would have imagined. It did not feel suffocating in spite of the hood and face mask.

"Follow me," a muffled voice emanated from Colonel Biswas.

They walked in a single file and emerged from the enclosure on the side of the desolate village. They walked up the gravel road for about 100 yards. Arthik's pulse quickened as he started to recognize some of the landmarks of his village. As they walked on, the road split. Colonel Biswas pointed to the right, and everyone followed. Houses lined either side of the street. There was no sound except for the muffled breathing within the face masks. Stray dogs looked up curiously at the hooded figures. Arthik recognized the homes now. His mind imagined the people who were there before, alive and well. Some sitting on the porch outside, kids playing in the street in the suffocating heat.

He shook his head. He had to stay focused. His house was not far now.

"I want to go to my house, Colonel," Arthik said, looking at Colonel Biswas.

Colonel Biswas nodded. "Lead the way."

Arthik picked up his pace, as the gravel road gave way to a paved street. The number of roaming stray dogs grew. A pack of about 10 dogs followed them at a safe distance.

"This was the central place in the village. Like a town square," Arthik said.

They came upon a wide area, where two other streets converged. Shuttered shops stood all around. The storefront signs were dusty, but still legible—General Merchants, Saree Palace, Bicycle Repair, Barber Shop. An empty commuter bus straddled the middle of the road, with a huge Bollywood billboard on its side. Faces of movie stars, with their vacant Velcro smiles, stared absurdly at the desolate landscape.

All four of them paused as they looked at the signs. They took in the stark silence for a minute, reminded of the terrible tragedy that took life away from this village in such a gruesome manner.

Arthik closed his eyes and hung his head.

Colonel Biswas put his hand on Arthik's shoulder, and squeezed through the layers of the protective covering.

"Let's go to your house, Arthik," he said.

Arthik looked at him and nodded. "How come the dogs are not affected?" he asked, pointing to the stray hounds following them.

"This virus does not infect dogs. We have taken random samples, and they are all negative. And a lot of times, animals act as carriers, but are not infected by the virus."

"Do we still have to wear all this stuff? Everyone's dead," Arthik said. There was a tinge of bitterness and anger in his voice.

"It might not be necessary, but we are not sure. Until we understand the life cycle of this virus, we have to take precautions," Colonel Biswas answered, his voice soft.

The road split into two small streets. Arthik turned right, and stopped in the middle of the road. He was staring at a house down the street.

"That your house?" John asked, his voice like an echo from within the confines of the face mask.

Arthik nodded. He didn't trust himself to speak.

Everyone stopped and stood by him. They realized this moment's infinite significance for Arthik.

"Let's go," Arthik mumbled after a few long moments. For the first time, he was thankful for the face mask.

CHAPTER 19

ARTHIK WALKED SLOWLY TOWARDS THE SMALL house. It had a wraparound three-foot wooden fence, splintered at a few places. From the dusty, half-paved road, a stone path led up to the house. Arthik's heart pounded as he leaned against the fence. He hung his head and said a short prayer for his family. He swallowed hard and slowly walked up the steps toward the front door. His brain conjured up images from times past. His grandfather sitting on the porch, his sister skipping in the front yard, her pigtails bouncing, his parents arguing in the kitchen about what to cook for dinner. The face mask suddenly felt suffocating, and he felt he couldn't breathe. He knelt and took a few deep breaths.

"You okay?" Kranken's voice came from behind him.

Arthik nodded. He stood up and pushed the door. A brood of hens flew out as soon as the door opened. The cackling was deafening.

"What the—?" Arthik almost fell back on John, who was right behind him.

The hens ran across the yard into the street. The pack of dogs that was following the group broke out in a barking frenzy. After a moment's hesitation, the dogs ran after the awkwardly scampering birds. All the hens were white. The dogs caught up and tore the hens apart. Feathers and flesh flew. Some hens scattered and half-flew, half-ran into homes along the street. The dogs growled over their spoils and ravished the remains. All this transpired in less than 30 seconds.

The group watched the macabre scene unfold, almost in morbid fascination.

"What the heck just happened?" John said, as he got up.

"Where did these hens come from?" Colonel Biswas said.

"My grandfather had hens as pets," Arthik said.

"Pets? You mean he had them in a coop?" Colonel Biswas said.

"No. Not in a coop. These were his pets. Nineteen of them," Arthik said.

"Really?" John asked.

"Yeah. He had names for each one of them."

"They all look the same, don't they?" Colonel Biswas asked.

"To us they did. But he could recognize each one of them. These hens followed him wherever he went," Arthik replied.

"We need to round up a few of these and run some tests on them," John said, looking at Colonel Biswas, who nodded assent, and got busy on his CB radio.

"There might be more inside," Arthik said, as he pushed open the main door again and waited a few seconds. No hens flew out this time. He stepped into the house and was immediately awash with nostalgia. He was in the living room of his old home. The furniture was the way he had left it. It didn't seem that it had been a year since he had left. An empty feeling filled his being. He walked into the dining room, leaned against the dining table, and hung his head.

"Which was your grandfather's room?" John asked.

Arthik looked up and pointed down the hall. "Second door on the right," he replied.

John walked down the narrow hallway, lined with hanging picture frames on both sides, and gently pushed the door open.

Another brood of hens flew out of the room and attacked John amidst the loud clucking and flapping wings. Some hens flew straight to his face. John staggered back and slid down the wall. One of the glass frames fell on his head, and the glass shattered. A piece of glass, about six inches long and three inches wide, came down like a dagger, cutting the neck of one of the birds and then went through John's protective suit and impaled in his right leg. The slayed hen's blood splattered all over his suit, and blood gushed from his injured leg. The rest of the birds dove back into the room.

Arthik came running over and started to drop on his knee.

"Stay back, Arthik," John shouted. "Stay back…. Get the Colonel here." He reached across and pulled the door of the room shut, locking the birds in.

Kranken appeared at the end of the hallway. "What the hell happened? More birds?" he asked, pointing to the shut door. A muffled cacophony emanated from behind the closed door.

"Stay away from me. My protection is breached," John repeated and winced with pain as he tried to move his leg.

Just then Colonel Biswas came in. It took him two seconds to take the scene in, and he bent down by John.

"It's okay, John. Your protection is breached, but mine isn't." Colonel Biswas went down on one knee, took a towel out of his pocket, and wrapped it around the jagged edge of the glass and pulled it out in one clean move.

"Agghh…" John groaned through clenched teeth.

Colonel Biswas put pressure on the leg for a couple of minutes and applied a tourniquet to stem the flow of blood. He looked up at Kranken. "Get one of the soldiers here." His voice was surprisingly calm and firm.

"Yes, Colonel," Kranken said.

Kranken and Arthik stepped back into the kitchen as the soldiers came in and made arrangements to move John to an isolated treatment unit at the base camp. The process was efficient and quick. John gave a thumbs-up sign as he was carted off on a stretcher.

"I hope he is okay," Arthik said. The incident had left him shaken.

"He'll be fine," Kranken said. "Maybe these birds will have some answers."

Just then, Colonel Biswas walked back in.

"How is Dr. Eters, Colonel?" Arthik asked him.

"So far, so good. He is contaminated with that sliced hen's blood. I don't know what that means right now. Tell me about these hens and your grandfather." He pointed down the hall, from where the faint cackling still permeated through closed doors.

"He had these hens as pets. He had nineteen of them. All of them were white. They followed him around. He would feed them, carry them, and occasionally some would sleep in his lap."

"These hens had a place…like a coop or something, where they would lay eggs?"

"Yeah," replied Arthik. "In the backyard. I had a lot of those eggs."

"Did you eat them too? The hens, I mean—" the colonel asked.

"No. Never ate the hens as food. He was protective of them, I guess," Arthik replied.

Colonel Biswas was lost in thought for a moment.

Kranken, who had been a quiet listener, asked, "You think these hens might have something to do with this disease?"

"I don't know. Their beaks are really sharp. We are almost certain that your grandpa was our index case. Maybe they poked him. Or cut him while eating from his hand if he was feeding them himself. Lots of possibilities," the colonel said.

"You know something," Arthik said slowly, "grandpa always did have cuts on his hands, and these cuts would bleed occasionally. He was always looking for an antiseptic to put on the scratches."

"Yeah?" Colonel Biswas said. "There might be something there. We will look into it." He then gave orders to the soldiers to transport the remaining hens.

"Where will these birds be taken to?" Arthik asked.

"They will be taken to a secure area at the base camp. Maybe these birds have some antibodies that we can use in future outbreaks. I am headed to the camp now. Do you want to stay here a while?"

Arthik nodded. "I would like to spend some time here."

"That's fine. Just make it to the camp before the sun sets," Colonel Biswas said. There was no room for negotiation in the tone of his voice.

"No problems, Colonel," Kranken said. "I'll get him home in time."

Arthik relived his entire life in the next 20 minutes. Every minute was excruciatingly bittersweet. Each corner and crevice of the house flooded him with memories that seemed so recent, so fresh. And that made it ever so painful. He knew this pain would stay with him forever. His sister's room brought him close to tears. His picture with her still hung on top of her study table.

The suffocating heat did not bother him, as his mind dove into the web of his memory cells, flashing images of his sister. He looked at her partially made bed. It was so goddamn unfair. So young, so full of life, and such a horrible death. His thoughts froze for a second. It was the first time his mind had used the word *death* with any of his family members. His stomach clenched, and he quickly walked out to the hall. The walls of the house seemed to converge on him. He felt claustrophobic. He found himself on the patio in the rear of the house, leading onto the backyard. He had an urge to rip off his protective gear to breathe in the fresh air. He felt trapped. He had so many questions about how his family died. The patio furniture was still the way he remembered it. He sat on a chair and took a deep breath. His eyes fell on the footprint on the patio.

He bent down and wiped the dust with his gloved hand. He followed the trail of the footprints, a smaller footprint encompassed by a larger one, to the other end of the patio. He remembered that rainy day well, about two decades ago. Waves of nostalgia overcame him, and he dropped to one knee as he stared at the two-in-one footprints.

"You okay, Art?" Kranken's voice came over his shoulder.

"I am fine," Arthik replied, without looking up.

Kranken came up from behind him. "Those yours?" he asked, looking at the footprints.

Arthik nodded. He traced his finger around the larger footprint first. "My father." Then he traced his index finger all around the smaller one. "That's me, many years ago." The footprints seemed to have a personality. It was as if these footprints, engraved in the patio cement for over a quarter of a century, were calling out his name. As he stared at the footprints, his father's voice seemed to echo back at him.

"We all are okay, in a better place…you stay strong…"

Arthik got up and walked out of the house without another word. The echo of footprints followed him.

CHAPTER 20

THE BASE CAMP WAS BUSTLING AND SEEMED AS EFFIcient as before. It took 10 minutes to unwrap the protective gear. John Eters had been transported to the Post Graduate Institute of Medical Education and Research in Chandigarh, one of the premier medical institutes in India.

"How's he doing?" Arthik asked Colonel Biswas.

"Too early to tell," he replied. The creases on his forehead were more prominent. "Those goddamned birds. We never knew about those hens."

"It still might not mean anything," Kranken said.

"I hope you are right," Colonel Biswas said. "I hope for John's sake this disease has nothing to do with those hens."

"Where do you have all the birds now?" Arthik said.

"A few miles from here. We have them in an environmentally controlled tent. There were eight of them. Six white and two brown. We even have the two dogs who attacked and killed three of the birds in the same area. The security around that tent would impress the prime minister of India—"

"Did you say brown?" Arthik sat up, looking at Colonel Biswas.

"Did I say what?" Colonel Biswas asked, his brow furrowed.

"Brown. You said two of the hens were brown?" Arthik was towering over the colonel now.

"Oh, yes. Two of the hens are brown. You know, brown feathered," the colonel said.

"Well, my grandfather did not have any brown hens."

There was a short silence.

Kranken looked at Arthik. "You sure?" he asked. "Never?"

"I'm sure."

"Somebody else in the village could have a brown hen. Or he could have got a new one since you left—"

"No." Arthik's tone was final. "It was considered a curse to have a brown hen. It's been a tradition in our village since the ages. Nobody in the village would keep a brown hen. If you have brown hens in that tent, they don't belong to our village."

The silence this time was a bit longer.

Kranken was standing now. He stepped closer to Arthik.

"Are you sure of what you just said?" Kranken asked.

"I am sure." Arthik did not flinch.

Kranken ran his hand through his hair. "I need transport to get back to the hotel. Not a word of this to anyone. Got it?" His eyes suddenly seemed colder. Almost lifeless.

Arthik just nodded, not trusting himself to speak.

"What do you think is going on?" Colonel Biswas asked.

"Nothing good, Colonel. We had reports of suspicious activity and chatter from across the border, just prior to this outbreak."

"I will need to inform the security people—"

"With all due respect, Colonel, let me handle that. I have direct access to the Indian CBI chief. I will call him. This has to be kept securely under wraps. If this suspicion turns out to be well founded, then the last thing we want to do is tip off the terrorists."

Colonel Biswas nodded. "Your transport will be outside in two minutes. The driver will stay with you for the rest of your trip. I must go to work on those hens." He hurried out of the tent.

A seething rage built up inside Arthik. His hands clenched to keep them from shaking.

"Do you really think this was deliberate? Like an attack?" Arthik's voice was calm.

"I don't know, Art. It's possible, but I'm not sure," Kranken replied.

"If it was deliberate, who is responsible?" Arthik's voice was strained now.

Kranken looked at him for a long moment. "We don't know anything at this time, Art. These are just suspicions. If I do find out something, you will be the first to know."

Arthik nodded.

"Are you coming with me to the hotel?" Kranken asked him.

Arthik nodded in assent, still not trusting himself to speak.

Back at the hotel, Ricky and Monty were waiting in the lobby.

"I have some info, Chief," Ricky said. "And I don't know what to make of it."

"Let's go into our room," Kranken said. "Art, you rest up and I'll catch you later."

"I want to be in on this," Arthik said.

Kranken shook his head. "It's too dangerous, Art. The less you know, the safer you will be—"

"You think I care about myself now? I have lost everything. I have nowhere to go," Arthik paused.

"I understand, Art, and I am sorry—"

"You couldn't possibly understand," Arthik interrupted. "My world came to an end when this outbreak occurred. If this was intentional, I want to know who did this and then my life's mission would be to end theirs. So please keep me in the loop." Arthik's eyes stared back.

Kranken looked at Arthik for a long, searching second and nodded.

"Thanks, Joe," Arthik said.

"Just one thing," Kranken said, looking straight at Arthik. "Whatever we talk about, whatever you hear, whatever we do, is just between us. If anything leaks or gets out because of you, I will kill you. I would hate to do it, but I would not have any choice, would I?"

"No, you wouldn't," Arthik said, swallowing hard.

"I wouldn't what, Arthik?" Kranken's voice was ice cold.

"You wouldn't have a choice but to…to kill me," Arthik said.

"You understand that?"

"I do." And Arthik believed it.

"Let's get working on this," Kranken said, and started towards his room. "So, what do you have, Ricky?" he asked, as he opened the door to his room.

"Well, Chief, there seems to be a lot going on," Ricky said, as he settled on the sofa. Kranken waved Monty and Arthik to sit down.

"Our guy McKay had a rendezvous with a gentleman at the Aroma café in sector 22," Ricky continued. "I was able to get a good seat and great pictures of both of them. I ran the face identity profile with some help from my friends in DC. It turns out that the gentleman in question is Ahmed Balochi, a second-tier leader of a separatist outfit, based in Kashmir. He is on the Indian government's most wanted list."

"He has some balls, to be in a place crawling with Indian security forces," Monty said, as he started to download pictures from Ricky's phone.

"He is smart. He knows everybody is busy trying to contain the outbreak here," Kranken said.

Moments later, a face popped up on the screen.

"Gentlemen, I give you Mr. Balochi," Monty said, as he adjusted the resolution of the picture.

The monitor showed a clean-shaven man, crewcut short hair, in about his early thirties, with piercing, intelligent eyes. It was a pleasant face that you wouldn't forget easily. It was a face you would trust. But the passion in those eyes bothered Arthik.

"What happened at the café after they met?" Kranken looked at Ricky.

"They were studying a map for a while, and Balochi was explaining something to McKay, pointing to the map."

"How did you know it was a map?" Kranken asked.

"A hundred rupees goes a long way. The waiter at my table was a smart kid. He knew a little bit of English. He told me it was a map, and he also told me that it was a map of the USA. And there's more…"

"More?" Kranken said.

"Yes," Ricky's voice was tight. "The café has balcony seating, which looks down on the general seating area. I was able to get to that area and take pictures of the map they were looking at."

Kranken nodded. Ricky had all the cutting-edge gadgets, and powerful cameras were a part of his arsenal.

Ricky looked at Monty and nodded.

Without another word, Monty punched a few keys on his keyboard and a colored map of the USA showed on the laptop screen. Monty then zoomed on the Eastern seaboard and then further onto the Washington, DC, area. The whole area was circled with a black marker. There was a black dot to the west of DC.

"Close up on that black dot," Kranken said. The picture zoomed bigger, and the location of the mark became clearer.

"That's Loudoun County," Arthik said.

"That spot is about 30 miles west of Washington, DC," Monty said, superimposing a scale on the screen.

"What does this mark mean?" Arthik asked.

There was silence for a few seconds.

"Worst case scenario, that mark could represent the next strike area," Monty said in a quiet voice.

In his subconscious mind, Arthik had known this, but actual verbalization of the same made him catch his breath. He felt sick to his stomach, imagining the carnage this virus could cause in the congested suburbs of Washington, DC.

"Ricky, be McKay's shadow." Kranken's voice was clear and edged with a fierceness. "Don't let him out of your sight. Where is he now?"

"Here, in his hotel room."

"Monty, find out whatever you can on McKay. I want to talk to him later."

Alone in his room, Kranken dialed Gordo's number.

"Hello," Gordo croaked. It was very early in the morning in Washington, DC.

"Hi, Gordo, this is Joe."

"What's up, Joe?" Gordo was awake now. "Calling from a scrambled line?"

"Yeah."

There was another short silence. Kranken grinned to himself and waited.

"You sure?" Gordo asked, his voice hesitant.

"Yes, I am sure. Now if you have stopped shitting in your pants, can we talk about matters of national security?"

Gordo's heavy breathing came over the line.

"Let me ask you again. Who is Bill McKay?" Kranken continued.

Gordo's response took maybe a second longer than it should have. That's all Kranken needed. Gordo knew something.

"I think he belongs to biohazard—"

"Cut the crap, Gordo. I need to know. I have contacts in Washington too. I can start digging, and I will eventually find the answers. I called you to save time. McKay has been hobnob-bing with a suspected terrorist here." Kranken's tone was soft. "If you want me to do the job you sent me here to do, play straight with me."

"Okay, Joe, what did he do?" Gordo sighed.

"First of all, this outbreak here might not be accidental—"

"What do you mean?" Gordo was fully awake now.

"I am not one hundred percent, but I think this was inten-tional. Your suspicions were well founded. It seems somebody planted the bug. CDC can work on the how. I plan to find out who, and why. So, who is McKay?"

For a few seconds, Kranken only heard Gordo's heavy breathing.

"It's classified. I can't tell you who McKay really is," Gordo said.

Kranken smiled. Gordo was telling him something without really telling him.

"Well, I might have to ask him a few questions, Gordo," Kranken said.

"Well, Joe, I am pissed that they did not tell me who he is either. When you have the answers, please let me know too. And this conversation never happened." The line clicked dead.

I have the go-ahead to question McKay, thought Kranken. Not that I needed that, anyway. He glanced at the phone and smiled to himself. He punched a few numbers on the phone and waited. His replayed his entire conversation with Gordo, then dialed Monty's number.

"You got something on McKay?" Kranken asked.

"Yeah, some. He's a decorated ex-Seal. Lots of missions in Afghanistan, but then something strange. Since about five years ago, it's like he fell off the grid. P.O. Box for an address, no credit card transactions, no utility bills. Nothing. It's as if someone is constantly wiping his prints from the face of the earth."

"Driver's license?"

"None on this name that matches his age. But listen to this," Monty continued, "the only thing that has come up on a web page is that he has been a contractor with IPBW."

"What the hell is IPBW?" Kranken asked.

"Institute for Prevention of Biological Warfare," Monty said.

There was a short silence as Kranken digested this info. "Where is this institute located?"

"Washington, DC," Monty replied.

"An ex-Seal working for the Institute for Prevention of Biological Warfare," Kranken mused aloud. "Find out whatever you can about this IPBW. I think it's time we had a talk with McKay. Come down to the lounge."

CHAPTER 21

KRANKEN KNOCKED ON MCKAY'S DOOR. MONTY AND Ricky stood on either side of the door jamb.

As soon as he heard the click of the latch turn, Kranken kicked the door with all his strength. As the door flew open, Monty and Ricky moved in quickly and stood over McKay, as he lay on the floor, his hand covering his bleeding nose.

"What the fuck—" McKay started.

Kranken stepped in, shutting the door behind him.

"Hush, Mr. McKay. The dramatic entrance is just to make sure you understand that we are serious and mean business." Kranken's voice was soft and cold, like an ice water droplet splashing on your bare back. He signaled to Monty and pointed to a laptop on the table.

"Who are you?" McKay asked, trying to get up.

"Arms above your head," Ricky said sharply, helping him up. He felt something over the left breast pocket and pulled out a Glock from a shoulder holster. "Any more teeth, my man?"

"He's clean now, Chief," Ricky said, after patting him down. He pushed McKay onto a couch.

"You don't need to worry about who I am, just tell me who you are," Kranken said, in the same tone. He grabbed the other chair and pulled it directly across from McKay.

"I am Bill McKay, biohazard sec—"

"Don't insult my intelligence, McKay. I don't have much time, so I will ask you again. Who are you working for?" Kranken continued in the same soft, menacing tone.

"We are on the same side," McKay said, looking down at the floor.

"Look at me," Kranken said.

McKay looked up into those ice-cold eyes.

"If we are on the same team, then tell me who you answer to in Washington," Kranken continued.

"If I don't want—"

Kranken's right hand smacked the left side of McKay's face before he could finish. The force of the blow left him sprawled on the floor, with a split lip.

"You were saying?" Kranken said slowly, rubbing his right hand.

"You guys don't know who you are messing with—"

Kranken kicked McKay in the stomach.

"Aagh…" McKay groaned.

Kranken grabbed McKay's shirt, pulled him up, and then threw him back on the chair.

"Listen to me, you punk," Kranken hissed. "I can make you disappear and nobody would have a clue. So either you tell me what I want to know, or I send for a body bag."

McKay looked into the ice-cold gray eyes, and felt a chill down his spine.

"You are all too late," he whispered.

"Late? Late for what?" Kranken asked.

McKay breathed heavily. He coughed and spit up blood.

"For the big show in Washington. The wheels are already in motion," he said.

Ricky bent down low and put his face close to McKay's. He put his hands around his neck. "What show in Washington?"

"They will kill me if I tell you anything," McKay said, getting his breath back.

"And I'll kill you if you don't," Kranken said. His voice was matter-of-fact.

"I think he has a meeting today. Don't you, Mr. McKay?" Monty said from the back of the room. He had been working on McKay's laptop.

McKay kept silent and looked quickly at the floor. But for the first time, Kranken noticed a flicker of fear in his eyes.

"I'll ask you for the last time. Who is your contact in Washington?" Kranken asked. A gun appeared in his hand, and he shoved the muzzle into McKay's mouth. Blood poured out of McKay's mouth as his two front teeth broke.

McKay mumbled something incoherent.

Kranken pulled out the gun from McKay's mouth, and took a step back.

"What did you say?" Kranken asked softly.

"Raymond Colling—" McKay started and then a red blot appeared on McKay's forehead and he slumped forward on his chair. The sound of breaking glass followed microseconds later.

"Sniper!" Ricky yelled, and everybody hit the floor. But there were no more sounds of shots fired, only a distant rumble of a vehicle speeding away. Kranken looked at the slumped McKay on the chair from his vantage point on the floor. The eyes still had that flicker of fear, but were glazing over as McKay stared into eternity.

Ricky got up and rushed to the side of the shattered window. He had his gun drawn as he peered outside. There were high-rise buildings across the narrow street from the hotel.

"Hundreds of windows right across," Ricky said. "Could have been any one."

"We are slipping. Fuck me…," Kranken said, shaking his head. "We should have covered that goddamn window. Monty, get his laptop and anything else that might help us dig a little deeper. Ricky, get me Colonel Biswas. Clean this up and keep it quiet."

Colonel Biswas listened patiently to the details of what had happened. He asked a few questions here and there.

"So what agency did this McKay work for?" he asked.

"We really don't know, but it points to an agency called the Institute for Prevention of Biological Warfare," Kranken said. He could sense that the colonel was upset.

"Mr. Kranken, there are a few things we can conclude from all this. First, this outbreak, which has killed about five hundred people so far, was not accidental. Secondly, there are more attacks planned, and third," Colonel Biswas paused for a quick second. "An official agency of the United States may be involved." A vein pulsed prominently on the colonel's forehead.

"I agree with all that you have said except the last bit," Kranken said. "No official US agency could be involved in this barbaric crime. A rogue agent, maybe. Colonel, the next attack is probably in Washington, DC, according to McKay. This was a trial run."

Colonel Biswas squared his jaw and shook his head.

"You are right. But it makes me very angry. So many innocent lives. For what?" Colonel Biswas said, his voice shaking.

"I know what you are saying, Colonel," Kranken said. "I want to catch these guys as bad as you want them. But not the small fish. I want the big cheese. That is the only way to stop the next attack. Keep this killing quiet. We will go to the hotel where he was supposed to have a meeting later today."

"What time was that meeting today?"

"At 5:30 p.m. Aroma restaurant in sector 22," Kranken replied.

"Those are exactly the people who probably shot him."

"Probably, but you never know. Maybe we will get a clue."

Colonel Biswas stared at his hands for a few moments. "Do you need any backup to go with you?" he asked. "That's the congested part of the city. A lot of people are still there, despite the tragedy."

"I appreciate the offer, but that will tip off the person there. My plan is to get more information about the next attack, if possible."

Colonel Biswas threw up his hands. "I will do as you say. You will have until this evening. Our undercover agencies will start working on this right now. The agents will be careful to keep your cover intact. You will need somebody to go with you who can speak the local language—"

"Thanks, Colonel," Kranken said. "But I got somebody who speaks the local language."

Colonel Biswas looked at him with eyebrows raised, and then in a second, a smile touched his lips. "Ahh…you mean Arthik. I think he will do good. My undercover team will be about a mile away. Just call if you need us."

"Thanks, Colonel Biswas. I've got to call Washington now."

"The big show in Washington?" Gordo's heavy breathing came down the wire. "What the fuck did he mean by that?"

"Well, Gordo, earn your salary. Get your undercover agents working overtime on this. Check the online chatter and dig into this McKay, this biological warfare institute or whatever."

"Anything else you got from his laptop?" Gordo asked.

"Monty is working on it right now. If anything shows up, I'll let you know. We will check out this hotel where he is supposed to meet somebody. My team and I are going to fly home as soon as we can."

"The people he is supposed to meet probably killed him." Gordo echoed Colonel Biswas' thoughts.

"Probably. This whole thing is so screwed up, there might be more than one outfit involved," Kranken said.

"Be careful. I'll have a plane ready in New Delhi. Just get there in one piece. One question, Joe," Gordo paused. "What's your sense about this big show McKay was talking about?"

There was a short silence. Kranken knew why Gordo had asked that question. He wanted to know Kranken's gut feeling.

"I have a feeling this here was a trial run," Kranken replied. He had no hesitation in his voice. "I think they are planning to hit the Washington area."

The silence was a bit heavier and longer.

"Get your ass back here as quick as you can." The line clicked dead.

CHAPTER 22

LATER IN THE DAY, ON THE WAY TO HOTEL AROMA, Arthik had a lot of questions. Ricky was driving the SUV, and Kranken rode shotgun. Arthik and Monty sat in the rear seats.

"Somebody just shot him…just like that?" Arthik's voice had a touch of incredulity to it.

"Yes, just like that. The reason I am telling you all this is because I want you to realize how fucking serious this business is. You follow instructions to the letter. Don't question, don't think. Just do whatever we tell you."

"Whatever happened in my village was all planned? It was murder?" Arthik asked. His voice was quiet.

Kranken turned around from the front seat and looked at Arthik.

"Yes, Art, all the evidence points to it being an attack. But with McKay's involvement, we don't know who is responsible."

Arthik's jaw tightened, and his hands turned to fists. A deep burning rage took root in the pit of his stomach. He looked away from Kranken's piercing eyes. He knew he had to keep his morphing anger under wraps until he got close to the people responsible. Somebody had to pay for the death of his family and hundreds of others. *And they will,* he promised himself.

"You okay?" Kranken asked.

"I am okay," Arthik replied.

Kranken turned his attention back on the road.

"I don't know how you can drive in this traffic," he said to Ricky.

"It's a battle of wills and anticipation," Ricky said as he swerved to avoid a cow in the middle of the road. "You keep going, until someone gives way." He slammed his hand on the horn and kept it there.

After about another 30 minutes of driving through congested streets and chaotic traffic, Ricky pointed ahead.

"There's the restaurant," he said. He parked the car along the curb, about 100 yards from the hotel.

The bright red neon sign flashed "Hotel Aroma" at a quick, almost irritating pace.

Kranken turned around from the front passenger seat. "Take a good look at the picture of Ahmed Balochi. Ricky and I will go ahead. Arthik and Monty, stay twenty paces behind. Getting cover here is not a problem…it's very crowded. And Arthik," Kranken paused, to get full attention.

"Yes?" Arthik said.

Kranken took out a gun from his jacket pocket. "This is a Glock. It's loaded. You have fifteen shots. This is the safety. Turn it up, and this is ready to fire." He turned the safety on and off a few times.

Arthik took the gun without a word or change in expression, turned the safety on and off a couple of times, and slipped it into his vest pocket.

"I have a voice transmitter on me, and Monty has the receiver. In case we are separated and can't use the phone," Kranken continued.

Monty and Ricky were busy checking their handguns. It was a practiced drill in familiar territory for all of them.

Kranken nodded and stepped out of the SUV with Ricky.

After a couple of minutes, Arthik got out of the car with Monty and started walking towards the hotel. The path was lined with street vendors on either side. There were a lot of people, young and old, milling around.

The restaurant was crowded. Kranken and Ricky got a table at the rear right side of the rectangular room. Arthik and Monty walked in a couple of minutes later. They were able to get a table in about the middle of the room. There were about six tables between them. Arthik had a clear view of their table, and Kranken sat straight across from him.

"What can I get you, sir?" a waiter asked in clipped English, who had glided over silently.

Arthik glanced at the menu.

"You want something, Monty?" Arthik asked.

"Order a snack and a beer for me, please," Monty said, eyeing the main door of the restaurant.

"Okay. Two Kingfisher beers and a plate of samosas. Very mild spices," Arthik said to the waiter.

"Yes, sir. Coming up in a couple of minutes." The waiter glided away as silently as he had come.

Arthik looked around the restaurant. It was an upscale joint, with pictures of kings and maharajas adorning the walls, in elaborate, gold-plated frames. Bright red shaded lights hung low on each table, soft light reflecting off of the silver cutlery. The conversation around the tables was soft, as Hindi songs played in the background.

The waiter brought their order to the table.

"What's this stuff?" Monty asked, looking at the samosas.

"It's good stuff—" Arthik stopped in mid-sentence.

"Don't turn around," Arthik continued. "Two men just came up and sat down at Joe and Ricky's table," Arthik said, as he watched the other table from the corner of his eye.

Monty stiffened, but did not turn around. He took out the small black receiver from his pocket and kept it on the table. He turned the dial on.

"Stay loose, Arthik. Let's listen in," Monty said, his voice calm.

The two men had slid into the two empty chairs at the table. Ahmed Balochi sat across from Kranken and had a .22 Derringer in his hand, pointed straight at him. He covered it nonchalantly with a table napkin.

"Hands on the table, gentlemen. No sudden movements." It was a confident voice, with a thick Indian accent. He was well groomed, with a pencil mustache. He was draped in an expensive suit and had a polished air about him. "This is a tiny weapon, but surprisingly effective at close range. I won't repeat my instructions."

The gun moved a bit and was now pointed at Kranken's head.

Ricky put his hands on the table first, making sure his movements were slow and deliberate. Kranken followed suit and remained quiet. In these situations, it was best to listen and speak only when needed.

"There's a lot of men with me all around. So please don't try anything." Balochi looked around and seemed satisfied with what he saw. "I knew you would show up here, Mr. Kranken," he said.

Kranken's brain flinched. *He knows my name.* "How do you know my name?" he asked.

"Don't concern yourself with minor details." Balochi was dismissive.

"Here's how this will go down," Balochi continued in his thick Indian accent, but in perfect British English. "Rakki here," he pointed to the other man with him, "will get up and start heading out. Both of you will follow him, and I will be right behind you. Keep your hands by your side all the time, where I can see them. Any sudden, abrupt movement, and you die." His voice was monotonous and measured. "I want your hardware on the table now."

Kranken looked at Ricky and nodded. Both took out their handguns and put them on the table.

"Who are you, and what do you want from me?" Kranken asked. His voice was equally calm.

"Aha. I'll answer the second question first. I want you dead. You are not going to ruin years of planning and hard work. We are at a point of no return." He picked up the guns on the table and slipped into his coat pocket.

"Why did you kill all these innocent people in the village?" Kranken persisted.

Balochi sat back in his chair. "Don't get all holier than thou on me, Mr. Kranken. You have killed many in your time."

"I have, but only scum like you." Kranken's voice was calm, matter-of-fact.

"Scum like me?" Balochi shrugged. "You don't know me well enough to judge me. The people here were martyrs. They all died for a noble cause."

"If you mean the big show in Washington, we know all about it. That's not going to happen," Kranken said quietly.

Balochi froze for just a second, his eyes searching Kranken's face. Then his lips curved into a soft smile.

"You are bluffing, Mr. Kranken," he said. "Americans will experience firsthand what they dole out to the rest of the world. This conversation is over. Rakki, let's go."

Rakki was a tall man with almost shoulder-length hair. The loose T-shirt he wore could not hide his rippling muscles. He smiled and exposed an empty space that normally would have held two teeth on the upper jaw. He got up slowly and started towards the front door.

Six tables away, Arthik had to muster all his willpower not to turn his head as Rakki headed towards the door, followed by Kranken, Ricky, and then Balochi, who had his hands in his jacket pockets, one of them no doubt holding a gun. Arthik's hands were balled into fists. These were the men who were responsible for murdering his family. He wanted to rip them apart, from limb to limb.

"Hold tight, Arthik. Stay cool," Monty said, sensing Arthik's rage. "I can see them now walking out the door."

"Let's go, then," Arthik said.

"Wait," Monty said. A second later, two men got up from another table and started walking out towards the door.

Monty nodded, dropped 300 rupees on the table, and headed towards the door.

"We have to act before they get them into a vehicle," Monty murmured to Arthik as he walked towards the door. "Stay behind me."

Arthik nodded, anger welling up inside him like a tide. He wanted to hurt the people who had brought such pain and suffering on his family. He followed Monty, staying just a step behind him.

Both did not see two more men get up as they left the restaurant, following them outside.

As Arthik stepped outside the restaurant, his instincts took over. There were people milling all around, talking loudly, as locals in these parts normally do. His eyes fell on a bunch of wooden sticks laying on the ground by the main door, presumably to hold up the tarp to cover the patio in the event of rain. Each stick was about six feet long, made of solid wood, and two inches in diameter. He picked one up and hurried after Monty.

The two men behind Arthik and Monty closed the gap between them.

"Hey!" one of them shouted.

Arthik turned around and saw the two men closing in. One of them reached inside his vest.

"Arthik, step—" Monty started to say as he took in the situation.

"I got this, Monty," Arthik said, turning around and taking a long step towards the advancing men.

Arthik's pent-up fury boiled over. He took one more step towards the man in front, who now had a gun in his hand. One quick strike with his wooden stick sent the gun flying into the darkness, catching the man totally by surprise, and the next jab of the stick was straight to the throat. As the lead man grabbed his throat while falling to the ground, Arthik stepped over him while swinging his stick in a 360-degree arc at lightning speed and struck the man behind on his skull. There was a sharp, sickening thud as the stick made impact with bone and he fell without a sound and did not move. Arthik turned his attention back to the first man, who was on his knees, still holding his throat and trying to get up. Arthik kicked out his foot with all his strength to meet the face of the man on his knees, resulting in a sound that made Monty wince. The man slumped to the ground, bleeding from the side of his mouth.

All this activity took exactly eight seconds.

"What the fuck?!" Monty's eyes were wide open. "What just happened? What…who the hell are you?" He had stood rooted to the spot, while Arthik, who had pulverized two men in less than a dozen seconds, was as calm as could be.

"We need to catch up to the others," he said to Monty, who just stood there, trying to digest what he had just witnessed. People were starting to crowd around the fallen men, and pointed at Arthik.

"Okay," Monty said, shaking his head and slipping his Glock back into his pocket. "You know you have a gun, right?"

Arthik didn't seem to hear.

"These people killed my family," he said in a quiet voice. He spit on the two motionless men on the ground. Arthik turned around and started half-walking, half-running towards the receding backs of the group including Kranken and Ricky, about 50 yards ahead.

Arthik held the wooden stick close to his body. They both had to wade through a sea of people to get close to the group ahead, which seemed to be headed towards a couple of parked SUVs. There were a lot of people walking about in that area. The boisterous crowd noise covered the sound of their rapid advance. When Arthik was about five yards from the last person of the single file ahead, that person turned around.

Before he could realize what was happening, Arthik was almost on top of him, now holding the wooden stick horizontally in front of him with tight fists, like a weightlifter would hold the weight bar. He jabbed the stick, fast and straight onto the man's chin. Even in the ambient crowd noise, there was a crunching sound of the jawbone pulverizing, and the man fell to the ground. Monty, in the meantime, had stepped forward to face the next man in line, who had turned around, hearing the commotion behind him. That man had three to four inches and about 50 pounds on Monty.

Monty raised his gun and shot him in the knee. The man let out a scream and fell to the ground, holding his mangled knee.

Balochi had turned around and realized the situation in a second. He fired as he turned, hitting Monty in his left shoulder, spinning him to the ground. Monty's gun clattered away as he hit the ground. Kranken threw himself at Balochi's knees, and they both went crashing down. He then managed to roll over on top of Balochi and brought his elbow straight down on his throat. He followed it up with a punch to the jaw that knocked out Balochi cold. Kranken shook his head to clear it and retrieved the guns from Balochi's pockets and turned around.

"You okay, Monty?" Kranken yelled.

"I'm okay, Chief," Monty replied, his voice surprisingly strong.

Ricky, in the meantime, had stepped in front of Rakki, who had a 12-inch kukri in his hand now. Rakki's upper body lunged forward, the light from surrounding bulbs glinting off the serrated blade. Ricky stepped back and stumbled over Monty, dropping to the ground on his back. Rakki smiled and started to move in for the kill with his kukri raised. Just then, Arthik stepped in, with his wooden weapon pointed at Rakki, the end of the stick about an inch from Rakki's face.

"No, Arthik—" Ricky started.

"It's okay, Ricky," Monty said, raising his hand. "Just watch."

Rakki moved back slowly, a faint smile on his face as he watched the stick move in small circles in front of his face. But the expression on Arthik's face cautioned him. Out of the corner of his eye, Arthik saw Kranken raise his gun, pointing it at Rakki.

"I got this, Joe," Arthik called out to him, without taking his eyes off the kukri. "This bastard killed my family."

The steel in Arthik's voice made Kranken lower the gun, but he still kept it half-cocked.

"He is okay, Chief," Monty called out from where he was laying, repeating this time for Kranken. "Just watch."

Arthik stretched his neck in a slow, tight circle. A voice boomed in his head...

"You know you will take him down, Arthik. The only question is how."

Rakki yelled out a few choice curse words in Hindi and lunged at Arthik with the kukri raised. Arthik was nimble and side-stepped easily. He hit Rakki's forearm holding the knife with the lathi, with every ounce of his strength. The forearm snapped like a twig, and sagged at an awkward angle. The kukri clattered to the ground.

"Aagh..." Rakki cried out, staring at his broken forearm.

Arthik took a quick step forward and jabbed the stick hard into Rakki's solar plexus, which brought him to his knees. And then Arthik's stick moved like a windmill. Rakki's head bobbed like a huge ball on a string as it got hit multiple times. Arthik stopped after a few seconds, and Rakki, his head bloodied, eyes staring blankly into nothing, fell face forward slamming into the dirt, and didn't move. Arthik stood over the fallen man, taking in deep breaths.

There were people gathering around now, looking at the trail of fallen men. Ricky and Kranken seemed to be frozen in time, trying to comprehend the precise savagery of Arthik's man-to-man combat skills.

"I told you," Monty said, shaking his head. "He is something else."

"What…what just happened?" Ricky's voice trailed off.

Kranken came out of his trance. He grabbed Balochi's shirt collar and dragged him towards Monty and Ricky.

"You know you have a gun, don't you?" Kranken asked, grabbing Arthik by his arm.

"Why does everybody keep telling me that?" Arthik said, looking at Monty. "Are you okay?"

"I'm fine, Arthik," Monty said, as his face grimaced.

"Let's get to our truck," Kranken said.

By that time, Balochi had come around. Arthik and Ricky half-dragged, half-walked him, holding him not too gently on either side.

"Where did you learn to fight like that?" Kranken asked, looking at Arthik as he helped Monty towards the truck.

"I didn't learn to fight. I learned to defend myself. I took lessons in Gatka, an ancient north Indian martial art form," Arthik replied.

"Well, you are damn good at it." They got to the truck and Kranken pushed Balochi onto the backseat. "Take care of him, Ricky."

"With pleasure, Chief," Ricky replied and proceeded to tie and gag Balochi.

"Colonel Biswas?" Kranken was on the phone. "We are outside Hotel Aroma. Monty got hit on the shoulder. We need to clean up here."

"I am sending in our Rapid Response team as we speak," Colonel Biswas said. "They should be there in five minutes. Start moving towards the base camp. The extremists will have backup in the area." The line clicked dead.

"Let's go, Ricky," Kranken said. "Watch out for any suspicious movement—"

In the next instant, the world turned upside down—literally. A midsized truck rammed their SUV, flipping it on its side, and the truck continued to push. The SUV, amidst screeching metal, burnt rubber and smoke, completely turned over.

Arthik found himself lying half outside the overturned vehicle. His head pounded, and he tasted his own blood. There was a searing pain along his left arm. Through the mental haze and actual smoke, Hindi speaking voices filtered through.

"Get Ahmed out...burn the truck...the army will be here in a minute..."

Arthik tried to raise himself up on his knees as he heard the doors being pried open.

"...make sure Sharma burns with all of them...no more use to us now..."

Sharma?

Even in the mental fog, Arthik heard his name crystal clear. It was like ceramic smashing onto a concrete floor in the middle of the night. Were they talking about him? But then survival instincts took over. He knew he had to get out of the burning SUV and get the others out too. A Molotov cocktail smashed through the window, and flames started to devour the fabric inside the vehicle. Arthik kicked the half-mangled door, and crawled out of the vehicle as the fire grew. He saw the truck that rammed them speeding away. He got to his feet and looked around for others. A person lay to his right, a few feet from the burning SUV. He staggered over and rolled the body over. It was Ricky. Arthik knelt down. He heard the soft breathing.

"Thank God," Arthik murmured to himself and dragged Ricky to a safe distance from the vehicle.

He hobbled back to the burning SUV. He saw Kranken's face, upside down, scrunched up against the passenger-side window. The door was remarkably undamaged. Arthik pulled on the door handle. It didn't budge. The rear end of the vehicle was now engulfed completely, and the heat singed the skin on his face. Arthik picked up a brick and smashed the window. He reached his hand inside and opened the door from the latch inside. He pulled Kranken out and dragged him away from the burning vehicle.

Ricky had come around by then, and looked about, clutching his right arm.

"Where the heck is Monty? MONTY…" Ricky called out. Sirens wailed at a distance.

Without a word, with adrenaline pumping, Arthik started running back to the burning SUV.

"Stay back, Arthik. It's gonna blow—" Ricky yelled.

And it promptly did. Arthik was about 10 feet away from the vehicle when it blew up. The force of the explosion lifted him up and threw him on his back. Arthik slipped into the bliss of nothingness.

CHAPTER 23

WHEN ARTHIK OPENED HIS EYES, HE SHUT THEM
again quickly as the bright light hurt his pupils. His head was
pounding, like somebody was sticking a hundred needles in his
brain, and each one generated its own epicenter of stabbing pain.
He heard voices. Somebody was calling out his name. The voice
seemed to be coming through a long and narrow tunnel.

"Hey, Arthik, open your eyes," Colonel Biswas said.

Arthik complied. He saw the colonel bending over him.

"Stick your tongue out."

"Where am I?" Arthik asked, his voice came out as a whisper.
"My mouth is so dry."

"We'll get you some water. You are at the Army Hospital
in Chandigarh."

Arthik pressed his forehead with the palm of his hands, trying
to relieve the pounding in his head. And then it all came flood-
ing back.

The SUV flipping over, the fire…

"Where's Monty?" Arthik asked.

"I think you need to rest, Arthik," Colonel Biswas was gentle as he pushed Arthik back on the bed.

"Where is he?" Arthik repeated, his voice almost a whisper. The intense throbbing of his head seemed better if he spoke softly.

Kranken stepped forward and stood by Arthik's bed.

"You were very brave, Arthik. I know you saved my life." Kranken's voice was quiet. Grateful.

"Where is Monty?" Arthik persisted.

"He was in the SUV when it blew up."

There was a momentary silence.

Arthik pressed his closed eyes with his hands and shook his head. He let his head drop back on the pillow, and squeezed his eyes shut, trying to get rid of the hammering in his head. Images of the vehicle rolling over flashed through his brain.

"I should have pulled him out," Arthik mumbled.

"There was nothing more that you could have done," Kranken said. "You rest up now."

The pounding in Arthik's head reached a crescendo, but the voices he had heard after the crash were clearer now.

Make sure Sharma burns with all of them…no more use to us now…

That kept on reverberating in his brain, amidst the pounding. Were they talking about him? *No use to them now…* What in the hell did that mean? Did he imagine that?

"Goddd…," Arthik whispered, trying to clear his head.

"We are leaving for Washington tonight." Kranken's voice pierced through his muddled brain. "You rest up here. We have to figure out the place and timing of the possible attack."

"Do you have any leads at this time?" Colonel Biswas asked.

"No. Balochi's picture has been sent out to all agencies worldwide. He is a hunted man. We don't have any other leads—"

"They were talking about me," Arthik interrupted, his tone quiet, but firm. "I mean, the terrorists. They mentioned my name."

There was a pause for a long couple of seconds.

"What was that, Art?" Kranken asked, his head cocked to one side.

Arthik's head was a lot clearer now. The pounding persisted, but the enormity of his realization kept the headache in the background.

"I heard someone say, *'got Ahmed...make sure Sharma burns with all of them...he is of no use to us now,'*" Arthik said.

"Is he delirious?" Kranken asked, looking at Colonel Biswas.

"I'm not sure," Colonel Biswas said.

"I'm not delirious. I know what I heard," Arthik said, holding his head in his hands. "How did they know my name?"

Kranken was quiet for a moment. One could almost hear the wheels in hyperdrive racing in his brain.

"Arthik, are you sure you heard what you think you heard? The SUV had just flipped over. Are you certain?" Colonel Biswas asked.

Arthik nodded. "I am sure. I heard those words quite distinctly."

"I don't know what the connection is, Arthik, but you just got yourself a ticket to Washington tonight," Kranken said.

Kranken stepped out of the room and pulled out his phone. He dialed Gordo's number.

"What's happening, Joe?" Gordo said.

"We need to fly back to Washington tonight. They got Monty," Kranken said.

There was a short silence.

"I am sorry, Joe."

"Yeah," Kranken said, taking a deep breath. He then filled Gordo in with the rest of the details.

"This makes no sense. How would they know his name? Are you bringing him to Washington?"

"Oh, yeah. You bet."

"The plane will be ready in New Delhi tonight," Gordo said.

Ricky, in the meantime, had gone ahead to New Delhi. He went to MIH, the Military Institute of Health, where John Eters was being treated. John Eters had been moved there from PGI, Chandigarh.

Ricky put on the contact isolation garb and talked to the resident doctor outside John's room.

"How is he doing, Doctor?" Ricky asked.

"Are you Joe Kranken?" The doctor was polite.

"Oh, no. I am Ricky Smits. I am on Joe Kranken's team."

"I am Dr. Sinha. Dr. Eters has been asking for him. He did not tell me the reason why. He is not doing well. High fever, low blood pressure. The skin rashes have not started yet, though." Dr. Sinha shook his head.

"Can I go in to see him?" Ricky asked.

"Sure."

Ricky stood by the bedside. John's eyes were closed. His face was a pale shadow compared to his ruddy glow from just a couple of days ago. IV lines pierced his arms on both sides. Nasal cannulas went into both nostrils, pumping oxygen. The cardiac monitor blinked above the bed, its steady tone oddly reassuring. White linen covered him up to his chest. The steady drone of the outflow fan hummed in the background.

"Hi, John, how are you?" Ricky asked, his voice muffled through the medical mask.

John's eyes opened, and a flicker of recognition crossed his eyes. He gave his friend a faint smile.

"Hi, Ricky," John said, his voice weak.

"Hang in there, buddy," Ricky said. "You are going to get better soon."

"I don't think so." John's smile got a little wider. "I need your help."

"My help? Sure. How?" Ricky said. *Is he delirious?*

"You found Arthik in three hours. I need you to find a person for me. Dr. Rupani Kapoor."

"Dr. Rupani Kapoor? Who is this?" Ricky asked.

"Somebody I let get away a long time ago." John's lips relaxed again into a faint, sad smile.

"Where is she?" Ricky asked.

"Here," John said.

"Here? You mean in New Delhi? Not in the States?"

"I mean somewhere in India. Can you do that for me?" John said. His voice was weaker now. "Her picture is in my wallet."

"I will. If she is on the grid, if she has a cell phone, if she has a credit card, I will find her. A date of birth or approximate age would—"

"March 7th, 1979," John interrupted.

Ricky looked at him for a quiet moment and nodded. He did not want to ask John any more questions.

"Let me get working on this then," he said. "I'll get back to you as soon as I can."

Ricky made a few phone calls as soon as he got out of the hospital and then headed to the United States Embassy in New Delhi.

Ricky apprised the Counsel-General at the embassy of the happenings at Majra briefly, without any mention of a possible attack in the States.

"Please don't mention any of this to anybody," Ricky said.

"Which agency do you work for?" the Counsel-General asked. He looked worried.

"The less you know, the better off you will be," Ricky smiled. "I need a secure computer and some privacy."

"Yeah, sure. This way."

It took Ricky less than an hour to locate Dr. Rupani Kapoor. She was in a city called Ludhiana, in the state of Punjab. She was currently an Associate Professor in the Department of Infectious Diseases at Dayanand Medical College. He went through her work history and saw she had worked in University of Maryland Hospital a few years ago. He looked at her cell number flashing on the screen. He thought for a couple of seconds and then reached for the phone on his desk.

"Hello? This is Dr. Kapoor," a strong, clear, confident voice answered at the other end. There was hardly any accent.

"Hello, Dr. Kapoor. My name is Ricky Smits, and I am calling from New Delhi," he said.

"Yes?" The voice was impatient now.

"Dr. John Eters asked me to call you," Ricky said.

There was a long pause.

"Eters?" Dr. Kapoor cleared her throat. "John Eters?" There were numerous unasked questions in the tone now.

"Please bear with me, Dr. Kapoor. I am calling from the United States Embassy. I am a part of the CDC team to investigate the outbreak in Majra. John is the field team leader for the scientific team and—"

"Why didn't Dr. Eters call himself?" Rupani interrupted. The voice was crisp again. She seemed to have recovered from her initial surprise.

"He didn't call because he is sick. He got the infected in the hot zone."

There was an audible little gasp, followed by a short pause.

"Where is he?" Rupani asked.

"MIH. In the ICU," Ricky said. "Would you be able to visit him?"

"They won't let me into MIH without clearance."

"I'll take care of that. Your name and ID will be at the gate," Ricky said.

"What is John's treatment protocol?" Rupani asked.

"I am sorry I don't know. I am not a physician."

"You are not? I thought you are with the CDC team—"

"Security. I am with security and logistics. Look for a Colonel Biswas when you get here," Ricky said.

"I'll start from here in the next hour." The line clicked dead.

Ricky stared at the phone and shook his head. He then called Colonel Biswas.

Somber faces gathered outside the ICU at MIH.

"How does John know Dr. Rupani Kapoor?" Colonel Biswas asked Ricky.

"I really don't know. John and she have a history together, from a few years ago," Ricky replied. "John asked me to find her. Considering his situation now, I think we at least owe him that much."

"We do," Colonel Biswas nodded. "I went over her professional history. She has very impressive credentials. She should be here any moment."

"How is John doing?" Arthik asked.

"Not good," Colonel Biswas said.

"Prognosis?" Kranken asked.

"There's a less than five percent survival rate with this infection. We are planning to infuse him with the serum from the survivors…that's his only realistic chance," Colonel Biswas said and left it at that.

A nurse came over to Colonel Biswas and handed him a chart.

"This is Dr. Eters' chart. There is a Dr. Kapoor at the nurse's station asking for you, Colonel."

"Oh, yes, send her here. We've been expecting her," Colonel Biswas said.

"Yes, Colonel."

A few moments later, a woman in her late thirties walked up to the group. She was tall, slender, with flowing dark hair, black piercing eyes, a strong jaw, full lips emblazoned with bright red lipstick, and an air of confidence that only a few carry. She had the kind of face that made you look twice. It was difficult to take your eyes away. The tight blue jeans and the semi-loose soft green top accentuated her curves.

"Hi, I am Dr. Kapoor," she said, in a clear, throaty voice.

"Hello, Dr. Kapoor. I am Colonel Biswas."

Introductions went all around.

"Thank you for coming, Dr. Kapoor. I called you from the embassy," Ricky said.

"Thank *you* for letting me know," she replied.

"Well, we will leave for the airport now. We've got to get back to Washington. You take care of John and help him pull through," Kranken said.

"We will try our best, and good luck to you too," Colonel Biswas said.

Kranken nodded and headed towards the exit with Ricky and Arthik.

"So how is Dr. Eters doing, and please call me Rupani," Dr. Kapoor said.

"Not good," Colonel Biswas said. "He has a persistently high fever, floats in and out of consciousness, his white count is high, electrolytes are stable for now, blood pressure is holding up, but barely."

Rupani was quiet for a long moment.

"Not looking good, is it?" she said, almost to herself.

"No," Colonel Biswas replied.

"How did he get infected? Breach in protocol?"

"Freak accident," the colonel replied and detailed the accident at the house when broken glass pierced John's thigh.

"Almost like a direct inoculation," Rupani said, and hung her head.

"There's one ray of light, though," Colonel Biswas said.

Rupani raised her eyebrows.

"We are giving antibiotics, antivirals, antifungals. Nothing seems to be turning this around. There is five percent of the population that was exposed, but not infected. There was this old man in the hot zone, everybody in that town just knew him as Seeti baba. He claims that he was going in and out of the village through a tunnel during the outbreak, and was looking after the sick people, taking care of them. And he did not get sick."

"Inherent immunity?" Rupani asked, her voice tinged with hope.

"Seems like it," Colonel Biswas replied.

"I presume you have isolated the B cells from him. How soon until we can infuse the serum?" Rupani asked.

"Hopefully tonight," Colonel Biswas said, rubbing his hands. "I hope to God that turns him around."

Rupani was quiet for a moment.

"It will," she said. "I want to see him now."

"Of course," Colonel Biswas said. "And one more thing, Dr. Kapoor."

"Yes?"

"I have arranged temporary privileges for you at this Institute. You are now the physician in charge of John's care. Is that okay with you?"

"You can do that?" Rupani asked, taken aback.

"This is a national emergency. So, is it okay with you?" Colonel Biswas repeated.

"Yes, it is. Thank you," Rupani nodded.

A few minutes later, she stepped into the room, wearing the protective isolation suit. She felt herself catch her breath as she looked at John. His eyes were closed, his skin pale. Multiple IV lines ran into his body. A dark stubble was starting to darken his face, with peeks of white hair in between. The reassuring, repetitive beep of the cardiac monitor droned in the background. A flood of memories flashed through her mind. The realization that he was more likely to die than survive made her a little unsteady and she put a hand on the bedrail for support. Her eyes moistened. The confident, strong façade was vulnerable. She was thankful for the face mask.

"John?" she said, the tone a little hesitant.

There was no response.

"John?" She was a little louder this time.

John's eyes opened, and his head turned slightly. His eyes tried to focus and he attempted to ask a question, trying to sift it through the face mask.

"It's me, John," she said, and her gloved hand found his.

John's lips curved into a smile, and it touched his eyes.

"Thanks for coming. You've been doing okay?" he said, the voice coming out as a hoarse whisper.

Rupani gave John's hand a gentle squeeze.

"I've been okay. What have you gotten yourself into?" Rupani said, her voice straining a bit.

"I was an idiot," John said.

"You sure were, to get into this situation—"

"No…not this," John interrupted. "I was an idiot to let you go. I'm sorry. You probably have kids by now—"

"I'm single, John. Hush now." It was Rupani's turn to interrupt. Even in a situation this dire, she could not help but smile.

John was exhausted with even this much effort. His closed his eyes and sunk into the bed. Rupani, the physician, took over. She scanned the monitors. John seemed to fall into a deep and restful sleep.

"I'm not going to let you die," she murmured to herself. She headed out of the room to look for Colonel Biswas.

CHAPTER 24

GORDO RUBBED HIS HANDS AND TOOK A DEEP breath. As usual, all 350 pounds of him was squeezed into a regular chair. Sweat poured down the sides of his forehead, and he kept wiping his face with a 6 x 6 white handkerchief. He looked at the three men sitting across from him. They had been whisked from Andrews Air Force Base as soon as they landed, to a nameless, faceless building in northern Virginia.

"I'm sorry about Monty," Gordo said.

Kranken nodded, as his hands formed firsts. "Makes me want to nail these bastards even more before they hurt anyone else," he said. The voice was as cold as his eyes.

Arthik felt the familiar chill along his spine every time he looked into Kranken's eyes. *Thank God I'm on his side.*

"You think this threat is real?" Gordo asked, looking at Kranken.

"I know it is. I saw it in Balochi's eyes. If they are able to pull it off, thousands will die…at least," Kranken said.

"And this gentleman…Arthik, isn't it? How in the hell did they know your name?" Gordo asked. This time he was looking at Arthik.

Arthik looked up, but was quiet.

"Arthik is from the village that was hit with the outbreak. His entire family was wiped out. He pulled me and Ricky out of the burning truck. Saved our lives, on more than one occasion," Kranken said, his voice quiet.

"I had Arthik Sharma checked out in detail when I knew he was coming with you both. The 7-Eleven he worked at has closed-circuit cameras with digital recording. Two hoodlums came in to rob the joint a few days ago, and our man here annihilated them. You remember that, don't you, Arthik?"

"Yes, I do," Arthik replied. "I was not fighting, I was defending myself." His lips curved into a nervous smile. He shifted in his seat, obviously embarrassed.

"The owner of the store must have been very thankful you thwarted the robbery," Gordo said.

"Probably," Arthik shrugged. "I've never met the owner."

"You sure have," Gordo said, his eyes squinting. "I traced your movements, for the last few months. His name is Ajeet Kasu. You met him a few times."

"Ajeet is not the owner," Arthik said, shaking his head. "He knows the manager. He helped me get the job."

"He owns that 7-Eleven. And many more," Gordo said. "He's loaded."

"Loaded? You mean rich?" Arthik asked.

"Not rich. Wealthy. He is worth about fifty million dollars," Gordo said. "But all clean. He worked honestly and hard for his money."

"Fifty million?! You are confusing him with someone else," Arthik said, his eyebrows arched. And then suddenly, Arthik put his head in his hands. "This might explain the cash…" His voice trailed off.

"What cash?" Kranken asked.

Arthik was quiet for a moment.

"A couple of days before I left, there was an unmarked box delivered to the store. It was full of cash…hundred-dollar bills."

"How big was the box?" Gordo asked.

"Not that big. About 2 feet by 3 feet," replied Arthik.

"Where is that box now?" Ricky asked.

"Probably still in the store, if he didn't pick it up yet," Arthik replied, shrugging his shoulders.

"I'll have someone check on it," Gordo said, wiping his face. "But, anyway, the only real lead we have is Raymond Colling. The name McKay mentioned before he was shot."

"Anything on Raymond Colling?" Kranken asked.

"Not much. His wife died a few years ago. Terrorist attack while the couple was vacationing in Europe. Not much else."

"Hmm…" Kranken murmured. "No other leads?"

Gordo took a deep, labored breath and turned towards him. He raised his hands and shrugged. "We have Balochi's mug shot all over the country and Raymond Colling's name. Nothing else at this time."

"Tell me more about Colling. Anything?" Kranken asked.

"Nothing out of the routine. One thing we are checking out is a research center in Western Loudoun County, affiliated with this institute. He has made frequent trips to this facility recently, not that he didn't do that before. But the log shows more frequent trips in recent months."

"I need the address for this research facility," Kranken said.

"Whatever you need, Joe. Do whatever it takes to prevent this. My men are bound by certain rules and witch hunts that invariably follow catastrophic events. You and your men have no such restrictions." Gordo wiped sweat from his brow again. He took a long swig from his water bottle.

Kranken nodded. "I got you, Gordo."

For Arthik, it was surreal. Visions of his village full of dead and dying people flashed in his mind's eye. Here he was, in one of the most powerful countries in the world, and there was a chance of that very same human tragedy being repeated again. And all these powerful men with all their sophisticated equipment, resources, and technology, were almost helpless. His village in India never had a chance.

Gordo's phone buzzed. "Yeah?" he snapped. He listened for a few moments. "How big is the farm?"

He listened for a few more moments. "Seal the perimeter. Nothing goes in or out of that place without checking. Let me know if anything changes."

"Is that the research facility?" Kranken asked.

"Yes. Some unusual activity in the last few days. Lots of vehicles going in and out of that place," Gordo said.

"Do they have animals at the farm?" Kranken asked.

"I am sure they do. Lots of people have horses in that part of Loudoun County. Why the sudden interest in animals?" Gordo asked.

"What about hens? Do they have hens?" Arthik's voice was animated now.

"Hens? You mean chickens? I don't know." Gordo cocked an eyebrow.

"There is a suspicion that hens might be the carriers of this bug. We are not sure. Arthik's grandfather was the index case, and he owned a lot of hens. We are not sure what it means."

"Nothing moves in or out of that farm without our knowledge," Gordo said. "We need to get moving." He then looked at Kranken. "I don't know what you guys are gonna be doing. And I don't want to know. You have three cars waiting for you in the parking lot with a lot of toys in the trunk of each car. These cars are marked and will not be pulled over by cops. Let's make sure this outbreak does not happen here. Keep in touch," Gordo said. "And Joe?"

"Yeah?" Kranken looked at him.

"If you must pull the trigger to stop this thing, do it. We are talking about hundreds of lives. Maybe thousands."

Kranken nodded. "I'll pull the trigger when I need to," he said.

"One more thing," Kranken said, looking at Gordo.

"Yes?" Gordo said.

"Tell your men not to interfere with me or my team. Just tell them to stand down, no matter what." Kranken's voice was firm.

"You got it, Joe," Gordo said. "They will move only if you ask them to."

The three cars stood side by side, in one corner of the parking lot. They were the same make, the same color, and had the same nondescript appearance of unmarked police cars.

"Pick one, Arthik," Kranken said.

"What do you mean?" Arthik asked.

"You are going to enter back into your life. Park this car a block away from your apartment," Kranken said. He walked to one of the cars and popped the trunk. He pulled the mat to one side. An audible gasp escaped Arthik. It looked like a small arsenal. There were three handguns, a shotgun, a couple of round objects that looked like grenades, extra ammo for the guns, a variety of flares, and a few metal canisters, approximately the size of coke cans. All this was snugly fit in a cutout felt piece of the trunk.

"What's all this?" Arthik said, in a forced whisper.

"These are the toys that Gordo was talking about," Ricky said. "And like he said, the cops won't pull you over."

"Pick a gun and keep it on you," Kranken said. "This one here will be good for you." He picked up the Glock, snapped the safety, pulled back to look at the magazine, and then loaded it back.

"No. I'm okay. I'll leave them in the trunk," Arthik said.

"Yeah. Just give him a broomstick and he'll take down anybody," Ricky said, with a smile.

"Okay, let's split," Kranken said, his tone suddenly authoritative. "Ricky, go to the research facility on Snickersville Pike and check it out. Arthik, you enter your life again. Make up a story about how you got the car. I'll be checking on Colling. Keep in touch and report anything unusual. Anything," he repeated with emphasis.

"And Arthik," Ricky said, looking at him.

"Yes?"

"It'll be okay. Just keep that temper of yours in check. And be aware of your surroundings. I don't know what the heck to expect. If these guys are as good as they seem to be, any of us can be a target," Ricky said. "Including you."

Arthik nodded and shut the open trunk.

"Ricky, check with me every hour on the hour and Arthik, you chime in 15 past every hour. Text or call," Kranken said.

CHAPTER 25

ARTHIK PARKED A BLOCK AWAY FROM HIS APART-
ment. The car was nondescript, but the engine had a zing to it.
He had made good time. He pulled out his phone to call Marge.
He looked at his watch. It was 3:30 a.m.

"I'll call her in a couple of hours," he murmured to himself.

He picked up his bag and paused a bit as his eyes lingered over
the trunk. Should he keep the handgun on him?

He shook his head and walked up to his apartment. As he
put the key in the door lock, it swung open before he turned it.
His heart did a sudden flip, and he stood still for a second. The
hallway light flickered, creating an eerie glow. For a moment he
thought of turning back and calling Kranken. The images of his
family, his village, rushed through his mind. His jaw clenched.
He was going to check this out. The apartment was dark. Arthik
strained his ears to hear any sound. Nothing. He put his bag down
gently. The overpowering smell hit him as soon as he stepped in.

It reminded him of the foul stench in his village when rats were killed to protect the crops. Only here, there were no rats.

His flipped the light switch.

"What the fuck…" Arthik muttered, as he looked at what was left of his room. It seemed as if somebody had gone through every inch of his apartment with a pair of big scissors. There was paper, ripped carpet, shreds of sponge ripped out of cushions, and broken glass everywhere. He shut the door and walked quickly towards the bedroom, following his nose.

Avtar, or what was left of him, was strapped on a chair. There were no clothes on him and his skin was pockmarked with round burns, especially in the groin area. A stream of ant-like creatures were spread out on most parts of his upper torso, tunneling in and out of the lifeless body.

Arthik fell back to the living area, and threw up. He then fell to his knees, his head in his hands.

"Oh, my God…oh God…." Arthik mumbled, rocking back and forth. He fumbled for his phone and called Kranken.

An hour later, Arthik sat stone-faced in his car. His hands gripped the steering wheel on the stationary vehicle so tight, that his knuckles were pearly white.

"You okay, Arthik?" Kranken asked.

He got an imperceptible nod in response.

"So tell me about…is it Avatar?" Kranken prodded gently.

"Avtar. A-v-t-a-r," Arthik spelled out the name slowly, deliberately.

"I'm sorry. I understand he was your friend. Pull yourself together. His death proves that the attack here is imminent. Whoever came to your apartment was looking for something. He has been dead approximately twenty-four to thirty-six hours—"

"He was tortured. All those burn marks on his skin. He had no nails on his hands. His fingers were just a mess of blood. And those bugs…" Arthik's voice faded, as he shuddered involuntarily.

Kranken's face transformed into a grimace. He had hoped Arthik hadn't noticed the details that he just spoke of.

"I know. Can you think of anything that these people were looking for in your apartment?" he asked.

"No. Nothing I can think of. I want to know who did this to him," Arthik said, his voice surprisingly calm.

Just then there was a knock on the window. Kranken stepped out of the car.

"Mr. Kranken?" The tall, well-built man in a crisp suit was respectful.

"Yes," Kranken answered.

Arthik also stepped out of the car.

"Detective Ross, sir. Forensics. I was asked by my superiors to give you an update," he said.

"Thank you, Detective Ross," Kranken said. "What do you have?"

"Very bizarre situation, sir. I have never seen anything like this. The time of death was approximately twenty-four hours ago. Extensive torture. And these bugs. These…these flesh-eating spiders," Detective Ross paused, and swallowed hard. He was still visualizing the tiny spiders tunneling in and out of the lifeless body. He cleared his throat and continued.

"I took a picture of them and flashed it to our database. It's a variant of *Latrodectus geometricus*, also known as the brown widow spider, found mainly in South America. How these deadly, rare spiders ended up on this guy, I don't know. It seems they burrow only into living...." His voice was almost a whisper now. He cleared his throat again. "These spiders will burrow only into living cells initially," he finished.

Arthik felt the bile rising as his stomach knotted. "Avtar was alive when these spiders were tunneling into him." It was a statement, not a question.

"Thank you, Detective Ross. Please keep me updated if you find anything new," Kranken said. His tone was colder than usual, and Arthik knew there was something.

"I got to check something out," Kranken said, as soon as the detective was out of earshot.

"What is it?" Arthik asked.

Kranken looked at him for a moment, and then seemed to reach a decision.

"Raymond Colling. He is a PhD in Immunology, Microbiology & Entomology and runs a research lab. He would have access to all kinds of insects and bugs. I was going to check out his place anyway."

"I am coming with you," Arthik said.

"It could be dangerous—" Kranken started.

"I am coming with you," Arthik repeated. The finality in his voice left no room for negotiations.

"Get in," Kranken said, and pointed to his car.

On the way, Kranken called Gordo.

"You guys are staking out Colling?"

"Yes, we are," Gordo replied.

"Where is he now?" Kranken asked.

"At his home, in McLean."

"Text me his address and tell your guys to stand back. I'm headed there now," Kranken said.

"Anything new?" Gordo asked.

"Yeah, possibly," Kranken said, and then went on to tell him briefly about the situation in Arthik's apartment.

There was a brief silence.

"The threat to Washington is real," Gordo said. It was not a question.

"It is."

"Fuck. You get moving. I have to brief POTUS and the Agencies," Gordo said. His voice was thick with worry.

Just then, Kranken's phone buzzed and a message from Ricky flashed. He was on his way to the research farm in Western Loudoun County.

Arthik pulled out his phone and dialed Marge's number. There was no answer.

"Whom are you calling?" Kranken asked.

"Marge."

"No answer?" Kranken asked.

"No. It's too early. I'll call her again in a bit," Arthik replied.

"Yeah. You do that. She lives close by?" Kranken asked.

"About fifteen minutes from here. Why?"

"Oh, nothing. Maybe you can see her after we visit Colling."

"Yeah. I'll do that," Arthik replied.

The house was majestic, even by the posh McLean standards. The night was dark and quiet at this early hour.

"That's a big house," Arthik murmured.

"Yeah. That's not on his salary. His wife was loaded," Kranken murmured as he strained his eyes to look for the stakeout car.

"The one killed in a terrorist attack?"

"Yeah. That's what probably turned him. There's the stakeout guys," Kranken said, pointing to a vehicle about 50 yards ahead on the straight road, among many others parked on the road.

"How do you know that is the one?" Arthik asked.

"The windows are fogged up. But they won't bother us," Kranken said. "Let's go."

There was no fence around the residence. Staying in the shadows, both made it to the back of the house. The water in the backyard pool lapped softly on the tiles, pushed by a gentle breeze. The pool was surrounded by lights spaced about six feet apart, casting a calming, soft light on the water.

There was a covered porch abutting the house. Kranken walked up stealthily to the door leading into the house from the porch. He pulled out a small flashlight and pointed it inside the glass-paneled door. It shone into a small room with green plants and light cane furniture. He reached into his pocket and pulled out a credit card sized, paper thin metal plate. It had a red rim that glowed in the dark

"What is that?" Arthik whispered.

"ESD—Electronic Sensor Deactivator. To deactivate the alarm on this door," Kranken replied. The device in his hand started to change color as Kranken started to scan around the edges of the door jamb. It froze to one color at a spot and Kranken gently pushed it in between the door and the door jamb. After a couple of seconds, the red rim changed color to green and then faded.

"Disarmed," Kranken said in a soft whisper.

He then took out a two-inch-wide, half-a-foot-long metal strip and gently inserted it into the slit in the area of the lock. In three seconds the door swung open. Kranken stepped inside, and Arthik was a step behind.

"Walk soft and stay close," Kranken murmured.

The sun room led into a family room. A night lamp was on. Light reflected off the glass panel of the fireplace on one side. The furnishing was sparse, and the carpeted floor swallowed the sound of their footsteps. The family room flowed into a small dining area. Light caught on the round, glass-top table and gave life to the wavy images from wall hangings around the room. Kranken held up a hand and put a finger to his lips. There were strains of soft music that caught the ear. Arthik pointed to a slightly ajar door across from the dining area.

As they moved closer to the door, the music got louder. It was soft, classical violin, playing to a fainter drumbeat in the background. Kranken pushed the door open ever so gently. There was no squeaking as the door swung open. Carpeted steps led down to the basement. A gun appeared in Kranken's hand as he started to head downstairs. It was a narrow stairwell and Arthik's heart jumped as he saw the picture frames lining the walls on either side. He tapped Kranken on the shoulder and pointed to them. There were about 8 to 10, boxed, square frames that lined the walls on either side. Each boxed frame was about six inches square and about three inches in depth. Every one of them highlighted a huge insect, about two to three inches in length, of varying color and shape, on a pearl white background. They almost seemed alive. And all of them, without exception, looked menacing.

Arthik's hands shook as he looked at the macabre images. He was sure this was the person responsible for Avtar's murder. As if in a detached subconscious thought, his mind wondered if he would find the bug that burrowed into Avtar's body on one of these frames. He shook his head clear, and followed Kranken down the stairs.

"You are too late, gentlemen," a voice boomed, as they both stood at the foot of the stairs.

They both spun around as bright lights came on.

A disheveled man, about 5 feet 10, stood behind a bar counter at the end of the huge basement hall. He wore big, round eyeglasses that seemed to cover more than half of his face.

"You can put the gun away. I am not armed," he said, as he walked around the counter. He wore a full-sleeved, bright green T-shirt, with black sweatpants. The tennis shoes he had on were neon green. His left hand wore a white golf glove. The walls of the hall were lined with hundreds of similar frames, each with an insect inside. There was a pool table on one side of the room. The cabinets behind the bar were open on the front end and seemed to be well stocked with a wide variety of liquor bottles.

The right side of the counter was lined with closed glass jars, about a foot high. Each one of them had what seemed like hundreds of bugs and insects crawling over each other. Even from a distance of about 20 feet, Arthik felt his skin crawl as his eyes fixated on the jars. The soft music from the ceiling speakers was starkly out of place.

"Care for a drink?" he asked, as he proceeded to pour himself a shot of bourbon.

Both Kranken and Arthik shook their heads, still trying to take in the bizarre scene.

"Raymond Colling?" Kranken found his voice.

"You got it," Colling replied.

"What do you mean we are late?" Kranken asked.

Colling looked at them both and smiled. "You are not here to rob me, are you?" There was nothing pleasant in that smile. "Which agency do you work for?" he continued.

"What do you mean that we are late?" Kranken repeated. The icy coldness was creeping back into his voice. Arthik could not take his eyes off the creepy, crawly creatures in the jars.

"Please don't insult my intelligence. I am impressed you guys got here. But as I said, it's too late. The wheels are in motion." And he took a large gulp of his drink, his gloved hand holding the glass. "You guys sure you don't want a drink? You look as if you could use one." His voice was calm.

Arthik was able to pry his eyes away from the glass jars.

"What does he mean?" he asked, looking at Kranken.

Kranken lowered his gun and walked towards Colling. "Why?" he asked. "Is it because of your wife?"

Colling froze and, for the first time, the nonchalant facade seemed to crack. His hand trembled.

"Let me pour you another drink," Kranken said. He walked close to the bar, and poured Colling a generous shot of bourbon.

"They killed my wife," Colling said. His hand was steady now, his voice without emotion.

"I know," Kranken said. "The bad guys did. Not the folks you will hurt if your plan goes through."

"There have to be sacrifices made to get to the big fish," he said. His eyes had a malignant gleam now.

"Why did you kill Avtar?" Arthik spoke up, rage oozing in his tone.

Colling looked at the towering Arthik, who had taken a few steps closer to him. His eyebrows furrowed for a moment and then something seemed to click.

"Aha. You are that Indian boy. The *Punjabi Gabru*. You should have died in India," Colling said.

Arthik paused in mid-stride.

"How do you know me?" Arthik had an unpleasant feeling in his gut.

"You survived," Colling said. "That's why your friend died. We were trying to find out if you had told him anything about the big show in Washington. But it does not matter now, we are at a point of no return. But you should have died, like your family did." Colling pointed his finger at Arthik.

Arthik stood still for a couple of seconds. He took another threatening step towards Colling.

"You are not making any sense. How do you know about my family?" His voice was calm, despite the anger behind his words.

"Hold on, Arthik," Kranken said. "He is our only lead."

"Well, my boy, it was so good you were here. We moved the hot zone to your village. We knew when you found out that your family was affected, you would rush there. We needed to get the passports and documents to our operatives there."

Arthik stood rooted to his spot, his brain trying to process the information Colling had just disclosed. His mind went into instant denial. It refused to accept that his presence in the United States was the reason his village was chosen as the site of the attack.

"How…how did I take your documents to India?" Arthik found his voice, albeit in a forced whisper.

Colling looked at Arthik and spread out his hands, his eyebrows arched.

"Did you take a bag that did not belong to you?" he asked.

Arthik stood frozen in time, for what seemed an eternity.

"What bag?" Arthik whispered the simple question, his mind blocking off the obvious answer.

"I think you know which bag. The one you couldn't find at the New Delhi Airport," Colling said in a whisper, mocking Arthik's tone.

Arthik put his head in his hands.

"But…Ajeet gave me that bag." Arthik's voice was low-key, riddled with confusion.

"Yeah. That bag," Colling said. "But I must say, the results were beyond my wildest dreams," Colling continued, oblivious of the blind rage that Arthik was building.

"Stand back, Arthik," Kranken said sharply, as Arthik lunged at Colling.

Colling jumped back, getting behind the bar counter, showing impressive agility despite his unathletic appearance. Arthik's mind was clear. He wanted to wring the life out of the despicable man in front of him.

And then Colling ripped open his shirt.

"Holy shit…!" Kranken exclaimed.

Arthik stood still as he took in the horrifying spectacle in front of him.

Colling had a bubble-wrap-like belt around his upper torso. There were spider-like, alive insects in each of the bubbles. His entire anterior torso seemed pockmarked with the bubbles, each about three inches in diameter. Enveloped inside each bubble were two to three spiders. There were tiny holes in each of the bubbles, presumably to allow air in for the spiders to breathe. The spiders had hairy legs, were about two inches in length, and were uniformly black in color. And all of these spiders seemed to be hyperactive, crawling over each other, and trying to get out of the polythene bubbles.

"You still want to hit me, you son of a bitch?" Colling screamed. "These are Brazilian wandering spiders—the most poisonous spiders in the world. I'll be paralyzed in 15 seconds after being bit, and dead in 30 seconds."

"Hold on, Colling. Nobody is going to touch you. Don't do anything stupid," Kranken said, holding up his hands.

Arthik raised his hands too and took a step back, away from Colling.

"Stupid?" Colling's voice rose to an even higher pitch. "*Stupid?* My wife was killed by these fanatics, and what did our government do? All these pompous politicians are cowards. Their vision extends only as far as the next election cycle. They care about nothing else. My wife was just a number to them. And they did nothing. NOTHING!" He was out of control. His eyes were wide open, and he was panting.

"What did people in my village have to do with any of this? Why the carnage there?" Arthik asked. His voice was quiet now. He could not take his eyes off the creepy crawlers inside the bubbles.

Colling was more in control now. He was breathing easier.

"We had to perform a trial run somewhere. And I had a lot of help from people who belong to that part of the world. And then you came along," Colling said. "We needed original documents to be hand-carried there by somebody totally clean, for our operatives to come to the United States. Your family and the rest of the people in the village made a sacrifice. They are martyrs."

Arthik was on his knees now, his head in his hands, rocking back and forth. The realization of what he had just heard hit him. He felt as if he was suffocating. His brain was working at warp-speed, trying to connect the dots.

"How in the hell do you know me or where I am from?" Arthik was able to get out between clenched teeth.

"It does not matter. You should have been dead, *Punjabi Gabru*. The real spectacle will be in Washington, DC. Attention will be focused back on the terrorists after thousands make the ultimate sacrifice."

"Sacrifice? That's murder. You will be no different than those who killed your wife. I promise you I can have every agency working to take out the people responsible for your wife's death if you call this off," Kranken said.

Arthik had been quiet, trying to make sense of what he had just heard. *Punjabi Gabru* reverberated in his mind. It didn't sound right coming out of Colling's mouth. The only person who called him by that name was Ajeet.

NO....!

Was that possible? He was the one who had given him the bag to take to New Delhi.

His mind was bruised from the leaps it was making to wrap around the information it was digesting. His stomach clenched at the implication, and he felt nauseous. It tried to limp back to the conversation taking place now.

Colling was speaking, and his voice was a little high pitched, but steady.

"It can't be called off. All operatives work independently of each other and have no connection to the world now. They will all complete their tasks in the overall mission. There is no way to get in touch with them. It's done." There was finality in Colling's voice. He was unnaturally calm.

The silence for the next two seconds seemed much, much longer.

"Ajeet. He is involved in all this," Arthik said, in a clear steady voice, surprising even himself.

"It doesn't matter anymore, *Punjabi Gabru*," Colling said, shaking his head. "You just happened to be at the right place at the right time for my plans. You are alive and that's why you are going through the pain of losing your family. It wasn't supposed to be like this. You should have died in India. I can understand your pain…I lost my wife. It has been hard. Very hard…" Colling's voice trailed off.

"Call this thing off, Colling," Kranken said, taking a step towards him. "There is no sense in killing hundreds more innocent people—"

"Don't take another step," Colling interrupted him, raising his right hand. "Like I said, it's too late now. It's done. I can't handle pain very well. And I know I won't be able to stand the interrogation. These spiders are hungry and will bite hard."

Colling put his hand in his pocket and pulled out a pocket knife. Before Kranken or Arthik could react, he sliced the front of his bubble wrap and the spiders scurried out. Colling stood straight and spread his arms outwards. His eyes and mouth were shut tight. A few spiders got to his neck and some crawled on his arms. Small pockmarks appeared where the spiders bit. Arthik and Kranken watched Colling's life ebb out of him, in morbid fascination. It was only a few seconds, but seemed an eternity. Colling stumbled a bit and then slowly slumped to the ground. His saliva drooled out, as the pharyngeal muscles were paralyzed. Then the rest of his skeletal muscles refused to obey neuronal commands. His eyes stayed shut, the chest stopped moving, and his mouth shaped into a permanent grimace. The spiders were still busy feeding on the now lifeless body.

"Fuck...!" Kranken exclaimed. "Let's get out of here before these critters start looking for more food."

Arthik didn't trust himself to speak. He just wanted to get out this house of horror. The framed insects seemed to close in on him as he scampered up the stairs. Kranken managed to pull out his phone.

"Get everybody here, Gordo. Colling is dead. Seal this place off. There are all kinds of weird, poisonous insects here." And he went on to give details about what had transpired.

In the next few minutes, the area was crawling with police cruisers, ambulances, and crews in biohazard suits.

"Your hands are shaking," Kranken said, looking at Arthik. "Tell me about the *Pan...Punjabi ga...* What was it?"

"Punjabi Gabru. It implies a young, vigorous, strong, Punjabi man. Ajeet is the only person who called me by that name." Arthik had a look of disbelief on his face.

"And he is the one who gave you that bag to take to India," Kranken said.

Arthik was still for a few moments, amidst the organized chaos of first responders. He leaned against the lamppost and looked at his hands. He clenched his fists to control the tremor.

"And that bag never showed up on the baggage belt at the New Delhi Airport. I thought the airline lost my luggage." Arthik's voice faded. He slid down to the ground and put his head in his hands.

"You know where this guy lives?" Kranken asked.

"Yes."

"Keep it together, Arthik. Let's go and talk to this friend of yours," Kranken said.

"I'm okay," Arthik said. "Just can't unsee what I have seen in the last couple of hours. First Avtar and now this." His voice trailed off as an involuntary shudder ran through his body. "They massacred my village because of me? I'm responsible for my family's murder?"

"Stay strong," Kranken said. "You are not responsible for any of this. We must focus on the job at hand to save hundreds. Where does this guy live?"

"Ashburn," Arthik said.

"Let's go to his place. Get in the car," Kranken said. "We will talk on the way. Where in Ashburn?"

"West of here, towards Leesburg," Arthik said, getting into the unmarked car. "Should I call him?"

"No. Let's surprise him," Kranken said dryly.

Arthik dialed Marge's number. After a few rings, the voicemail kicked in and he left her a message. "Hey, Marge. I'm back. Call me as soon as you get this message." Arthik hung up the phone and shook his head, trying to clear his muddled brain.

The car raced east on Route 7. Just then Ricky called.

"Anything new, Ricky?" Kranken asked.

"Nothing, Chief. Lot of vans came in and out of this research center over the last few days. That's from the security cameras. Nothing in here now, except for a bunch of jars and mice in cages."

"Go over the logbooks, notes, accounting books, whatever. Find an address or a name and pass it on to Gordo. We need a lead. I don't think we have much time left," Kranken said.

"Okay, Chief. This place is sterile. They cleaned it up pretty good, but I'll keep looking," Ricky said and hung up.

CHAPTER 26

"YOU THINK HE'S HOME?" ARTHIK ASKED.

They sat about 20 yards from Ajeet's home, in a suburban neighborhood of Ashburn. It was 6:15 a.m. The sun was just starting to peak over the horizon and trying to break the cloak of darkness.

"I don't know," Kranken said. "Let's find out. You have been to his house before?"

"Yeah, a couple of times," Arthik replied.

"You notice any security alarm system in the house?"

"I really wouldn't know," Arthik said, after thinking for a moment.

"Let's check his place out before people start waking up," Kranken said and got out of the car.

The house was set back in an unfenced, half-acre lot and had a stucco front. It was a pleasant, suburban home.

"Let's get to the rear. There's a door off the deck that opens into the living room," Arthik said.

They made it onto the deck, and Kranken ran his fingers along the edge of the door. He took out the credit card sized sensor again and swept it all around the door jamb. The lights flickered green on one edge and stayed that way.

"No alarms," Kranken said, as he pulled out a lock-pick. He inserted it into the lock and after a few twists and turns, there was an audible click as the latch released. He then gently pushed on the door, and it swung open. They both stepped inside the house.

It was eerily quiet. A car honked in the distance. Arthik pointed to the stairs that started from one end of the room, and mouthed the word "bedroom," with his finger pointing upwards.

A Glock appeared in Kranken's hand, and he went up the carpeted stairs. Arthik marveled at Kranken's agility.

At the top of the stairs, there was a small, wood-paneled area, surrounded by three doors. Arthik pointed to a double-paneled door—the master bedroom. Kranken gently pushed open the other doors first and made sure the rooms were empty. He came back to the master bedroom door and raised his Glock. He looked at Arthik and nodded. In one swift movement, he kicked the door open and stepped into the room.

"What the fuck…" Kranken exclaimed at the scene in front of him.

Arthik stood still, suddenly frozen.

The body of an African-American man lay spread-eagled on the bed, with hands and feet tied to the four bed posts. There were no clothes on the body. After the initial shock wore off, Kranken moved fast. He flipped on the light switch by the door and the room was cast in an earthy glow.

"Oh, shit… It's Keith!" Arthik exclaimed.

Kranken seemed not to listen. He moved swiftly around the room, kicked open the closet door and then another door, which led into the attached bathroom. There did not seem to be anyone else in the room.

Arthik went over to the bed.

"He's breathing," Arthik said, peering over Keith's motionless body.

"You know this guy?" Kranken asked, as he came over close to the bed.

"He is the manager of the store where I work." Arthik's hands shook, and he could hear his heart pounding.

Keith lay in a pool of his own blood. There were three distinct round, dark holes spread over the abdomen, the dried blood rivulets leaving a trail along the side of the abdomen.

"Cut him loose. I'll call the rescue squad," Kranken said, handing Arthik a small knife. "I don't think our friend Ajeet is here, but I'm going to check out the rest of the house."

"When is all this going to end?" Arthik said, as he leaned against Kranken's car, with his head in his hands. "You think Keith is going to make it?"

"No, probably not," Kranken said. "It ends when we stop this attack from happening. Put yourself in Ajeet's shoes. What is he thinking? Where is he now? Finding him is the only way we can stop this thing. Did he have any other friends?"

"Not really. Now that I think of it, he talked a lot about politics. He had some radical views. He was a cynic. Always complaining about the government. He believed the system was corrupt everywhere. But he was so generous, so friendly and helpful…"

"Did he ever mention what he wanted to do? To get back at the system?" Kranken asked.

"No. Not really," Arthik said after a moment's thought.

Kranken shook his head. "Get in the car, Arthik."

"I'm calling Marge," Arthik replied, as he got in the car.

A minute later, "Still no answer. Where the hell is she?"

"Her phone's probably off. Put yourself in Ajeet's shoes. Places you went with him. His favorite hangout spots. Where did he go to feel comfortable? Anything."

"I was at a couple of parties at his house. Most guests were of Indian descent. But he didn't have a high opinion of most of them, and I think the feeling was mutual."

"But he invited them to his home?" Kranken asked, his eyebrows arched.

"That's an Indian culture thing. You invite everybody and throw them all in a huge melting pot."

"Anyone close to him? Anyone he confided in?" Kranken persisted.

"Not that I know of," Arthik said, his voice trailing off. "You know something…."

"What?" Kranken asked, intrigued at Arthik's expression.

"He took me to the circus a couple of times," Arthik said, talking almost to himself.

"Circus? The real circus? Lion tamers and all?" Kranken asked.

"Yes, he had a thing for animals."

Kranken's phone buzzed.

"Yes, Gordo?" Kranken answered, and listened for a moment. "Homeless shelter? Send me the address. And Gordo?"

"Yes?" Gordo asked from the other end.

"Can you please find out if there is a circus playing in the Washington metro area?" Kranken asked.

"Yeah. The US Congress. It plays 24/7." Gordo's voice came over the line with the first hint of humor in days.

"Very funny, Gordo. I'm glad you haven't lost your ability to crack a joke. But I mean the real circus. With animals, acrobats, and all that jazz," Kranken said.

There was short pause. Heavy breathing spilt over the airwaves.

"A real circus? I'll find out. Why?"

"Long story. Just let me know," Kranken said and clicked the line dead.

"What's up?" Arthik asked.

"Well, one of Ajeet's cars was found parked outside the Leesburg homeless shelter."

"Leesburg homeless shelter? I went there with him a couple of times," Arthik said, sitting up. "I know where it is. Let's go."

As they sat in the car, Arthik called Marge again. There was still no answer.

"Where is she?" Arthik shook his head and looked at his watch.

"Where does she live? Maybe she's not awake yet," Kranken asked.

"She lives in Sterling," Arthik said.

"Is she the girl in the video from the store? When you almost killed those guys?"

"Yeah. I didn't hurt them that bad," Arthik replied, squirming in his seat.

"Not that bad? Apart from the movies, that was the most clinical exhibition of hand-to-hand fighting I've ever seen," Kranken said.

Arthik did not respond and tried the number again.

"She is still not picking up," he said.

"Don't worry Arthik," Kranken said. "Try again in a few minutes. She probably doesn't know you're back."

"Well, I did call her before we left India. She always answers her phone," Arthik felt a little restless.

Ten minutes later, as their car took the ramp for Sycolin Road, Kranken followed the array of flashing lights on police cars and emergency vehicles, as they all converged on the parked car.

"Is that an airport?" Kranken asked, as they passed an empty field with an airstrip in the middle. There was a variety of small single- and double-engine propeller aircraft parked along the side of hangar-like buildings.

"Yeah. That's the Leesburg airport. It's right across from the homeless shelter," Arthik said.

"Did he know how to fly?" Kranken asked.

"Ajeet? I don't think so. But I am finding out that I really didn't know him."

Kranken parked the car behind one of the police cruisers, and they walked up to Ajeet's car, which was now encircled with yellow police tape.

An officer came up to them.

"Mr. Kranken?" he asked.

"That's me," Kranken replied.

"I am Deputy Tanen, Loudoun County Sheriff's office. I was told to give you a report on the vehicle," he said.

"Thank you, Deputy Tanen. What do we have?" Kranken asked.

"Nothing suspicious around the vehicle, sir," Deputy Tanen replied. "As per instructions, we were waiting for you to get here to examine the inside. The vehicle does not seem to be booby-trapped." He stood stiff, and the tone was clinical.

Kranken looked at him for a moment. "I will only take five minutes, and then the vehicle is all yours."

He walked around the white Lexus SUV. There were no scratches or dents. Kranken put on latex gloves that the deputy handed him, and he opened the front passenger door. The vehicle seemed to be in mint condition. It even had that new car smell. He went over the back of the vehicle and opened the trunk.

Arthik paced up and down a few yards away. He whipped out his phone and dialed Marge's number again.

The sharp, clear, standard Apple ringtone cut through the morning stillness, over the hum of muted conversation and car engines. Arthik turned around towards the sound. It seemed to be coming from Ajeet's car.

Kranken reached under the rear seat and pulled out the still ringing iPhone. By that time, Arthik was right behind him.

"That is Marge's phone," Arthik said. He recognized the purple cover that they had bought together a few months ago.

"Right here, under the rear seats," Kranken replied. He knew what Arthik was going to say next.

"What does this mean?" Arthik said, his heart sinking.

Kranken didn't reply. He looked at the phone in his hand and then at Arthik. This was too easy, too simple. "You think she could be involved in all this?"

"What? Involved? All this killing…this shit? Are you fucking crazy?" Arthik's eyes blazed.

Kranken nodded absentmindedly, his mind racing far, far ahead.

"Ajeet has Marge," he murmured to himself. "She probably mentioned to Ajeet she had talked to you." Kranken looked at Arthik. "Did you mention anything else to her other than that you were coming home?"

"No. Nothing. I just said I am headed home in a few days. Nothing else." Arthik was calm now. He knew at that instant he would kill Ajeet. His rage channeled to a clear mind.

Kranken flipped open his phone and called Ricky's number.

"Yes, Chief," Ricky answered on the other end.

"Anything new on your end?" Kranken asked.

"Well, there might be something, Chief. I re-ran the closed-loop video circuit on all the computers here and the digital download on one of them survived. There were three closed box vans that left the warehouse around 3 a.m. this morning. It's a black and white video. The vans are dark, not black. And one more thing, there were a lot of empty spray paint cans—"

"Spray paint cans?"

"Yeah. The kind that are used by kids in schools. There were a lot of them in the garage. About twenty different colors. Bright colors."

"Painting the vans?" Kranken asked.

"Maybe. Why would you want your vans to stand out? These are bright, almost neon colors," Ricky said.

"Hmmm…." Kranken murmured.

"I don't like this, Chief. Anyway, I am going to upload the link of the video to Gordo's people."

There was a short pause.

"Yeah, do that. We need to get air surveillance to find these vans." Kranken then filled Ricky in with the happenings of the last couple of hours.

"And we came here to Leesburg, where they found Ajeet's car. He knows Arthik is back," Kranken concluded.

There was another pause.

"How do you know that he knows, Chief—"

"Because he has taken Marge with him to wherever the fuck he is," Kranken interrupted.

"Marge? Art's girlfriend, Marge?"

"The same," Kranken replied dryly.

"The kid can't get a break, can he? First his family, and now this," Ricky sounded pissed.

"Yeah, I know what you mean," Kranken said.

"Okay, Chief. You keep Art calm. If he loses his cool, he can really go nuts," Ricky said.

"Oh, yeah, I've seen that," Kranken murmured.

"Are we sure Marge is not on Ajeet's team?" Ricky asked, his voice hesitant.

"The thought did cross my mind, but seems unlikely. Found her cell phone in the SUV," Kranken replied.

"I don't like this, Chief." Ricky's voice was tinged with worry.

"Neither do I. I don't think we have much time, either. Things are coming to a head," Kranken said.

"I'm almost done here. I'll hook up with you in a little bit," Ricky said.

Kranken put the phone back in his pocket and turned around to see Arthik standing a couple of feet away. His jaw was clenched, and his eyes seemed to be looking far away.

"You okay, Art?" Kranken asked.

"Yeah, I'm fine." Arthik's voice was cold. "Whenever we catch up to him, he is mine."

Kranken opened his mouth to say something, and then he caught the expression on Arthik's face.

"Fine. But we have to find him first."

"We will find him. We have to find him," Arthik said.

"And soon," Kranken said.

He dialed Gordo's number.

"Yeah, Joe," Gordo answered. "What's new?"

Kranken ran over the past hour's events.

There was a short pause. Kranken could almost hear the wheels turning in Gordo's brain.

"He could have taken her anywhere. A chip to be traded later," Gordo said. "And what is this about spray paint?"

"I don't know, Gordo. This guy always seems to be a step ahead of us," Kranken said.

"We'll start looking for vans painted in neon colors," Gordo said.

"Why would he paint his vehicle in neon colors? It doesn't make sense," Kranken said.

"This guy is bat-shit crazy. Who knows why," Gordo said. "Oh…and one more thing."

"Yeah?"

"There is a circus playing in town. Loudoun County fairgrounds. Opens this evening. I don't understand the angle, though."

"We'll check it out. Probably nothing," Kranken said, and clicked the line dead.

Kranken apprised Arthik of his conversation with Gordo.

"A circus in town? We need to check that out later. I am going to Marge's apartment first," Arthik said.

"That's a crime scene now. I'll go with you. Where is her apartment?" Kranken asked.

"Sterling. A few miles from here."

Traffic was picking up now. Kranken turned on Sycolin Road to Ashburn and then towards Sterling.

Police cruisers were parked outside Marge's apartment building. A forensics team was going through every inch of her apartment. Kranken sensed Arthik stiffening as he walked into the apartment.

They were both asked to wear latex gloves before they could enter Marge's home.

Arthik walked around the familiar apartment. He had been here just a couple of weeks before. *Seems like a lifetime ago.*

"Anything interesting?" Kranken asked the officer in charge.

"Nothing right now. We just started. Haven't gone over the entire place yet. No forced entry, nothing broken inside the apartment. No booby traps so far. Nothing seems out of place. Strange pets, though," he replied.

"Pets? What kind of pets? Marge didn't have any pets." Arthik's stomach clenched.

"Hey, Warren," the officer called out. "Show these gentlemen what we found in the bedroom."

Warren walked out of the bedroom, with two hens in his arms, and a big smile on his face. Both the hens were brown.

For a moment, Kranken and Arthik froze. And then Kranken took over.

"Freeze, Warren," he said, in a clear, firm voice, his arms raised with palms outwards. "Don't anybody move. Warren, step back into the room, close the bedroom door, and stay there. Keep the hens in there. Anybody who came in contact with these hens, stay inside, and everybody else, step outside. Move…NOW!"

Everybody seemed to be taken aback by the intensity of Kranken's tone. Warren's smile contorted into a frown.

"But…what—"

"Just do as I say, Officer. I'll explain later," Kranken interrupted, and stepped back outside the apartment.

"Any more hens in there?" Arthik asked Warren before he closed the bedroom door.

"No." Warren was sweating now and was holding the hens as one would hold a ticking bomb.

"I…I touched the hens," an officer in the room mumbled, holding his hands up high.

"Step inside the bedroom. And you don't have to raise your hands," Kranken said, his voice gentle. "Lock the hens in the bedroom. You two officers can wait in the living room for further instructions. Did anybody else have any contact with the hens?"

All the other officers shook their heads, negative.

"Do not bring anything from the apartment to the outside," Kranken said and led everybody out.

A few minutes later, the apartment complex was besieged with wailing sirens and teams in biohazard suits.

Arthik paced back and forth in the parking lot.

"Marge could be infected. I've got to find her," he said aloud, almost to himself.

"It's a possibility, maybe Ajeet too," Kranken said, leaning against his car. "Maybe he wants to die a martyr."

"No," Arthik said, his voice very matter-of-fact. "He is mine. We have to save Marge first."

Kranken looked at Arthik and shook his head. Here was this young man who had lost everything in the last few days. Fate was being very cruel.

"Yes, Art," he said. "You bet your ass we are going to save Marge." Kranken's brain raced. He pulled out his phone and punched a number.

"Colonel Biswas?" Kranken said into the phone.

"Joe?" Colonel Biswas answered.

"Yes, Colonel. How is John doing?" Kranken asked.

"He is better. I think he just might make it. The serum seems to be working. We are trying to replicate it in the lab." Colonel Biswas sounded relieved.

"Someone from the US embassy and the CDC will be contacting you in a short while, Colonel. We have possible exposure here. Show them all that you have, so we can replicate it here."

"There is active exposure? Good God…I'll start working on it right now."

Kranken then called Ricky and brought him up to speed.

Ricky was silent for a short moment as he digested the information.

"Oh, Jesus. This guy is a step ahead of us all the time…" he exploded.

"We will get him. Get in touch with your contact at the embassy in India. Have them contact Colonel Biswas. He'll direct them about what to do."

"Got it, Chief. I'm on it. I talked to Gordo earlier. We have air surveillance looking for dark Chevy vans with any kind of neon spray paint markings on them."

"Keep me posted." Kranken clicked the line dead and looked at Arthik, who had been very attentive. "What now, Art? Where is he now?"

"I don't know. The only other place to go now is to the Loudoun County Fairgrounds," Arthik said.

"Oh, the circus," Kranken murmured. "Why not. Let's go."

Loudoun County Fairgrounds is a 100-acre open space, right off Route 7, also known as the Leesburg Pike. There was a retail complex on the north end, known as One Loudoun, sprinkled with restaurants and coffee shops. There was no traffic at this early hour, and Kranken pulled onto the road leading to the entrance of the fairgrounds.

"There's the circus tent," Arthik said, pointing to the largest cone-shaped structure at the south end of the sprawling acreage.

"That's a huge tent," Kranken remarked, as they drew closer to the structure. Mobile trailers were spread out behind the tent. There was some activity around the trailers. The circus staff were waking up. They were going about the morning chores and getting the arena ready for opening night. There were cursory glances at the slowly moving car, but nothing more. People just went about their work.

"Well, we are here," Kranken said and turned the engine off.

"What now?" Arthik asked.

"Let's look around a bit. This place looks too goddamned peaceful." Kranken got out of the car and stretched his legs.

They walked past the unmanned ticket counters. The typical fragrance of animal fodder percolated in the light morning breeze. The entrance was a 20-foot-wide hallway, leading on to the main arena. The hallway stretched on for about 100 yards and was lined by empty animal enclosures on either side. The enclosures were fenced and had plaques on the outside, with names of the animals who would be in the enclosures at opening time.

Arthik read the names on the plaques aloud as they walked the hallway.

"Lions…Elephants…Ostriches…Llamas…Tigers…
Horses…Petting area with multicolored animals. This is a
huge circus."

"It sure is," Kranken said. "You've been to this circus before
with Ajeet, haven't you?"

"I don't know if it was the same circus, but it was at this site.
I came with him a couple of times. He used to spend a lot of
time here."

"Can I help you, gentlemen?" A voice boomed behind them.

They both turned around to see a tall, well-built white man,
in a flaming red suit and a top hat.

"Hi," Kranken said. "We are just looking around. I wanted to
bring a bunch of kids to the circus this evening and was checking
the place out."

"I am Zotamus Chekesky, Ringmaster for tonight's show. The
kids will love it. The show starts at 8 p.m., but the petting area and
the stalls will be open at 5. Please come over. Tell your friends. Do
you have any questions?"

"I think we are okay. Do you mind if we look around some
more?" Kranken asked.

"Not at all. Please take your time. Holler if you need something," he said. He tipped his hat and walked off.

"Very friendly," Arthik said.

"Too friendly," Kranken remarked.

"You always suspicious?"

"Most of the time. Keeps me alive," Kranken said, as he smiled.
The smile didn't touch his eyes.

They walked on to the main arena. It was oval, surrounded by a seating area, extending about 30 rows back. They looked around for another 15 minutes.

"Nothing here," Arthik said.

Kranken just stood there, running his hands through his hair.

"Well, I don't know what we expected to find here anyway. Let's head out," he said.

"Where to?" Arthik asked.

"I don't know. Ricky should be here soon. I'll call Gordo and see if there is anything on the air surveillance," Kranken said and pulled out his phone. He called Ricky first.

"Hi, Ricky, what's happening?" he asked.

"Hey, Chief. I'm headed in your direction. Where are you right now?"

"At the Loudoun County Fairgrounds."

"What's up there?"

"Circus. Opening tonight," Kranken said.

"Oh. The hen angle. Found any leads?"

"None."

"I'll see you there in a few," Rick said, and the line clicked off. Kranken then dialed Gordo.

"Anything new, Joe?" Gordo asked.

"Nothing at the circus. Any leads from air surveillance?" Kranken asked.

"Not a damn thing. No neon or spray-painted vans. Nothing," Gordo said, sounding tired.

"Where the fuck do we go from here?" Kranken asked.

"Just keep looking. Agencies will stay on high alert," Gordo said. "Get some rest. The serum is on its way."

Ricky drove over a few minutes later.

"Sorry about Marge, Art," he said.

Arthik nodded, without saying a word.

"We'll find her," Kranken said. His voice lacked conviction.

"I talked to the folks at the embassy in New Delhi. John is doing well, and he is insisting on returning. He will be on a chartered plane with the serum in the next few hours. His ex-girlfriend is coming with him," Ricky said.

"She is coming on the same plane? Does she have a Visa—" Arthik started to ask.

"This is a worldwide crisis. No red tape. The governments want a handle on this. She was treating John. The US government wants her here fast, just in case there is an outbreak in the States. But it's all hush-hush. Imagine the panic if this got out," Ricky said.

Arthik nodded. "Where the hell are you, Ajeet?" he murmured to himself and held his head in his hands.

"Let's get some rest," Kranken said. "We are all exhausted. There is a NSA safe house in the area. We can crash there for a few hours. Leave your car here, Ricky. We'll pick it up in the evening."

The safe house was in Brambleton, just a few miles from the fairgrounds. It was a nondescript single-family home, tucked away in a quiet neighborhood. Kranken punched in the code on the main door.

CHAPTER 27

THE INCESSANT RINGING OF THE PHONE WOKE UP
Kranken. For a few seconds, he was in a space gap. His mind was
a web of memories and thought flashes. And then the past few
hours zeroed into the present moment.

"Joe?" Gordo sounded frantic. Almost.

"Yeah?" Kranken said, a frog still in his throat.

"Hostage situation in Baltimore. Eleven gunmen have about
two hundred hostages," Gordo was breathing hard. Kranken
heard what sounded like a chopper in the background.

"Two hundred? Where?" Kranken was awake now.

"The Baltimore Aquarium. In the central hall. These guys are
professionals. They've already killed at least five people. They are
heavily armed and all of them are wearing suicide bomb belts."
Gordo was panting now. "And one of them is Ahmed Balochi."

There was a short pause. Kranken's brain was racing. His free
hand massaged his forehead.

"They have the bugs with them?" he said, almost thinking aloud.

"Probably. I am headed there now. We have the area cordoned off and the negotiating team is on site."

Silence spun down the wire.

"You still there, Joe?" Gordo asked.

"Yeah. I don't like this," Kranken said.

"Neither do I, buddy," Gordo said. "But we have something to work on and we have the sons of bitches contained. Maybe the belts they are wearing have bugs in them, like that freak Colling. The max casualty number would be two hundred to three hundred. I'll take that over a few thousand. I'll keep you posted."

The line clicked dead.

Gordo had almost sounded relieved. Arthik and Ricky were up. Kranken looked at his watch. It was almost 4 p.m.

"What's up?" Arthik asked, rubbing his eyes.

"Active hostage situation," Kranken said, looking out the window.

"Hostages? Where?" Ricky asked.

"Baltimore Aquarium. About two hundred to three hundred people. Eleven terrorists as of this moment," Kranken said, almost murmuring to himself.

"What's up, Chief? You seem distracted," Ricky said.

"Do these guys have the bugs with them?" Arthik was awake now.

"They probably do," Kranken said. He was quiet for a moment.

"What do we do?" Arthik asked.

"This is probably the big show Colling was talking about. Maybe they have the bugs in Baltimore with them. That would create an outbreak," Ricky said.

"Possible," Kranken said, rubbing his chin.

"Godddd…," Arthik said, holding his head in his hands. "So Ajeet is with them in Baltimore? And Marge?"

"We will know soon enough." Kranken's tone was quiet.

Arthik shook his head and raised his eyes heavenwards. He let out a long sigh.

"Let's go get my car from the fairgrounds," Ricky said.

"Get back quick and then let's head to Baltimore," Kranken said.

Arthik and Ricky reached the fairgrounds around 5 p.m. There were a lot of people milling around. Some adults were huddled in groups, talking in hushed tones. The news from Baltimore had spread. A few families were headed back out of the fairgrounds.

"I've never seen so many children in my life," Arthik murmured.

"I thought the show does not open until 7 p.m.," Ricky said.

"The food stalls and the petting area open early. At 5:00, I think," Arthik said. "I'm sure the kids are crazy about the animals here. Where did you park your car?"

"Just around the next turn, towards the right. The parking area behind the big top," Ricky said, pointing in that direction.

There were a lot of people on the driving path. The car barely crawled.

"You know what, it'll be quicker if I walk. You start turning around, and make it to the main gate and wait for me there," Ricky said.

"I'll park here. I just want to take another look inside," Arthik said.

"Okay, see you in a bit."

Ricky got out of the car and half-walked, half-ran towards the back of the big tent.

Arthik parked the car and strode towards the tent. He bought a ticket and headed towards the entrance. He walked the hallway, as he had earlier in the day. But it was crowded now. Adults and children stared at the animals in fascination. The air was filled with the typical circus smell, a mixture of animal excrement and fresh dirt.

The biggest crowd seemed to be around the petting area for the "Multicolored Animals." Arthik tried to stand on his tiptoes, to add inches to his six foot two inch frame. He got a glimpse of brightly painted small animals scurrying around with little kids running after them inside the enclosure. Just then, his phone rang. It was Ricky.

"Yeah, Ricky. I'll be out in a minute," Arthik said.

"Now. Come out now. Towards the back. Near my car." And the line clicked dead.

Arthik rushed out, scrimmaging with the crowd, and ran towards the back of the tent. He spotted Ricky standing next to a grey van.

"Is this one of the vans?" Arthik panted out.

"I'm not sure. The windows are all blacked out," Ricky replied. "But look at this." He pointed to the back. Arthik peered closely.

There were spots of bright paint, of many different colors—red, yellow, neon green, and pink—splattered on the running board of the van.

Arthik stood frozen for a few long seconds, staring at the bright spots of paint, as if transfixed by them.

"Fuck…fuuuck…." Arthik groaned and looked back at the entrance he had just emerged from.

"What is it, Art?" Ricky knew Arthik was on to something.

"All these people. The little kids in there. They are being exposed to that…that bug," Arthik blurted out.

"What? Exposed to the bug? How?" Ricky was confused.

"The multicolored animals in the petting area—I bet you there are a few hens in there." Arthik pointed to the paint spots on the van.

"Ohh, fuck…." Now it was Ricky's turn to look heavenwards.

They both looked at the entrance, now milling with people. Ricky fumbled with the phone and dialed Kranken's number. He put it on speaker phone.

"Yes, Ricky?" Kranken answered at the other end.

"We got a huge problem, Chief," Ricky said. "We found the van with spray paint spots on the running board, outside the circus tent. There's a petting stall with multicolored animals—"

"Oh, for fuck's sake. The situation in Baltimore is a decoy." Now it was Kranken's turn to groan. But in a second, he was in charge.

"How many people there?" he asked.

"About five or six hundred," Ricky replied.

"How many entrances to the parking lot?"

"Just one."

"Get to the main entrance that leads to the circus parking. Nobody leaves, and nobody gets in. I will have backup there ASAP. Recruit the officers on duty there. Not a word to anyone. We don't want panic. Get the petting area closed." The line clicked dead.

"Let's go," Ricky said. "Get the petting stall closed. I'll take care of the entrance."

"How do I get the stall closed without telling them the truth?" Arthik asked, trying to keep up with Ricky as they jogged to the circus entrance.

"Use your imagination. If that doesn't work, use this." Ricky pulled out a Glock.

"Whoa...I can't use this," Arthik was quick to reply.

"There are many ways you can use a gun without hurting anyone." Ricky shoved the handgun in Arthik's hand and ran towards the main parking lot.

Arthik looked down at the gun in his hand and pushed it into his waistband. He then rushed back into the circus tent. He pushed and clawed his way to the front of the petting stall. A continuous wail of sirens started to filter in, seeming closer every second. He felt his stomach clench as he captured the scene inside the petting stall. There were goats, pigs, sheep, ducks, geese...and hens. All animals had one thing in common. They were all spray painted in bright, neon colors. Small children, toddlers with their parents and grandparents, were inside the petting stall—touching, caressing, and kissing the animals.

"Oh, God...oh, God," he murmured to himself, over and over again. A prominent sign above the stall stating, "The spray paint used on these animals is PETA approved" mocked him. The sirens were louder now, and the crowd threw nervous glances at the entrance door.

In a flash, Arthik stepped in the stall, pulled out the Glock, and fired in the air. The noise was loud but was overwhelmed by the screams that followed. Adults grabbed their children and scrambled towards the exit. A couple of young, well-built men took a couple of deliberate steps towards him, but Arthik pointed the gun towards them and just shook his head. They promptly joined the scramble towards the exit. The area cleared out in a few seconds.

A harried, middle-aged woman wearing an official striped shirt had just come running from inside the tent after hearing the commotion.

"What's happening here?" she asked no one in particular. And then she saw the gun in Arthik's hand and her hands shot up above her head.

"My God! Don't hurt me…please…"

"I'm not going to hurt anyone. Just wanted to get this area cleared out," Arthik said, as he put the gun back in his pocket and pointed to the brightly painted animals scurrying around him.

"When did these hens get here?" he asked.

"This…this evening, a couple of hours ago," the lady replied, her lips trembling. She still had her hands above her head. The wailing sirens outside were very loud now.

"Who got these animals here?" Arthik asked, stepping closer to the woman.

The woman staggered back, and Arthik put his hands on her shoulders to prevent her from sliding to the ground.

"Who got these painted animals here?" Arthik asked again. This time his voice had steel in it. The sirens were louder.

"The supplier is still in there," the woman said, her voice barely a whisper. She pointed towards the interior of the big top tent.

"Still in there? Are you sure?" Arthik asked, his body stiffening up.

The woman nodded and pointed again towards the main arena.

"Just get out of here," Arthik said and stepped out of the stall, carefully locking the door, to keep the animals in. He pulled out his gun and headed towards the main arena.

CHAPTER 28

ARTHIK PULLED OUT HIS GUN AND WALKED SOFTLY towards the main arena. The hallway was about 50 yards long. It was semi-lit, with incandescent bulbs flickering along the way. The hallway opened up and split to lead to the various seating sections. Arthik stopped at the edge of the hallway, his heart in his mouth. He let his eyes adjust to the darker interior of the big top. The faint rumble of running footsteps filtered through. Arthik hugged the side wall and raised his head slowly above the bannister.

"Oh, crap…" The whisper escaped him, at what he saw.

About 20 yards away, sitting in the first row, on adjacent seats, were Ajeet and Marge. The rest of the arena, about a thousand seats, spread out around an oval performing area. It was empty. Their facial features were not clear, but Arthik knew. It was them. Marge seemed to be dozing off. Had he hurt her? A slow anger started to burn within. His jaw clenched and his hand closed tight around the butt of the Glock. Was there anyone else around, backing up Ajeet? But the rage welling up within him blinded good sense. He started to rise up to show himself.

"Don't move," a voice whispered in his ear. It was Kranken. "Is that him? And Marge?"

Arthik nodded assent, his jaw still clenched, as he crouched down.

"Then we must be very careful, so that he does not hurt her," Kranken murmured, his voice barely carrying to Arthik.

Ricky sidled up just then. He took in the scene in a couple of seconds.

"We could take him out with a single shot," whispered Ricky.

"No," Kranken whispered back. "He might be wired with explosives or bugs. Or she might be."

"And he might have help here in the hall," Ricky whispered.

There was a short silence.

"Let me go up to him, with my arms raised. He will talk to me," Arthik murmured. "Anybody else goes up to him, and we don't know what he will do."

Kranken shook his head. "Too risky. This is a cold-blooded murderer," he said. "He just might freak out seeing you and take a shot at you or something."

"I still have the best chance," Arthik whispered. "And that is the only way to save Marge. She is all I have left in this world." Arthik's eyes blazed.

Kranken took a deep breath. He had made a decision.

"Ricky, go back out and tell the feds nobody comes in here. Tell them it's a hostage situation. Then you come back here and lay low. I will be Arthik's backup, and you will be mine."

Ricky nodded and silently scurried back towards the entrance. "Put the Glock in your waistband, and go out with your hands raised," Kranken continued. "No sudden moves and keep him talking. Try to get him to let Marge go. Got it?"

"I got it." Arthik felt an icy calm enveloping him. He knew what he had to do. He raised his head slowly over the bannister to take a look. He then looked back at Kranken.

"Don't interfere with what I am going to do, Joe. He is mine to take down," Arthik whispered.

"Now don't do anything stupid—" Kranken started to whisper, but Arthik was already on his way towards Ajeet and Marge.

Arthik raised his arms above his head and walked at a measured pace. He was icy calm. He knew he was going to kill Ajeet today. He just had to figure out how to make sure that Marge did not get hurt.

"Hey, Ajeet," Arthik called out. His voice came out strong. He saw Ajeet straightening up in his seat, but Marge did not move. Arthik kept walking slowly, but deliberately. Faint light shone on them from the top of the cone-shaped tent. Even in that limited luminescence, he could see that one side of Marge's face was bruised, especially around the eye. His rage boiled.

Hold it together, hold it together. A voice cautioned from his subconscious.

"Arthik? Good Lord! You made it? My Gabru Puttar." Ajeet had a big smile on his face. But it didn't touch his eyes. His eyes darted around the arena, looking for answers to Arthik's presence.

"I did make it," Arthik said, now about 10 yards away. His hands were still high up in the air.

"How did you find me? Are you alone?" Ajeet was standing now. His right hand held a gun.

Arthik did not respond. His eyes focused on Marge. Her head rested on her left shoulder. The bruise on her face was clearer now. There was a small laceration on the left side of her forehead, with a dry rivulet of clotted blood snaking down the side. In the dim light, he couldn't tell if she was breathing.

"What did you do to her?" Arthik asked, without taking his eyes off her, his heart pounding.

Was she...?

"She was a handful. I had to subdue her. She is infected now, so...," Ajeet said, shrugging his shoulders.

Arthik tore his eyes away from Marge's face. The exhaustion was gone, the web of confusion regarding the events of the last few days was relegated to the background. There was clarity of the job at hand now.

"You killed my family. You took everything from me," Arthik said and moved a step closer. His voice sounded unnaturally calm. For a quick second, his mind fantasized about squeezing Ajeet's neck. Then, as quickly, he was back to reality.

"Why did you pick my village to attack?" Arthik's voice was strained but didn't quiver.

"Well, I needed to get passports and documents to India, for all my people to come to the US. You were the perfect vehicle. I knew you would go to India if your family was involved, my Gabru Puttar. You were the unsuspecting courier for the cause when you took my bags with you. It's a sacrifice—"

"It's murder. So many innocent people. You are a fucking monster," Arthik said, his voice firm.

"Your family and everybody else are martyrs. I will be too, and thousands of people infected here today. We all will die in a couple of weeks. This is an incurable disease. There will be a new world order," Ajeet said, his voice dripping with pride.

Arthik wanted to tell him that a potential cure was on its way from India right at this minute. But he wanted Ajeet confident, unperturbed, with his guard down. He took a step towards Ajeet.

"Don't take another step," Ajeet said. The gun in his hand was pointing at Marge now.

"Let me hold her. She is all I have left," Arthik said, his voice still even.

"You will get infected," Ajeet replied.

"You think I care whether I live or die now?" Arthik asked.

Ajeet looked at him for a long moment.

"Okay, my Gabru Puttar. For old times' sake, I will let you hold her. We can all be martyrs for this great cause. Keep your hands where I can see them. You know I won't hesitate to shoot." Ajeet stepped away from Marge, and kept his gun pointed in her direction.

"I know," Arthik replied. The rage inside him evolved into an icy, detached calmness. His mind had cleared a path. Make sure Marge was not wired and then take Ajeet down. A voice echoed in his head—

"You know you will take him down, Arthik. The only question is how."

Arthik kept his hands raised and walked towards Ajeet.

"That's far enough for now, Arthik. Turn around," Ajeet said.

Arthik complied, his hands still raised. Ajeet walked up behind him and frisked him. He relieved Arthik of the Glock.

"I'm sure there are people here with you, Arthik," Ajeet said.

"What people?" Arthik asked.

"The people who gave you this gun," Ajeet sighed. "It doesn't matter, we all will die in a couple of weeks anyway. Don't do anything stupid. Go sit with Marge now."

Arthik walked up to Marge and sat beside her. She seemed to be in a deep sleep. He cleared the wisps of hair along her forehead. He was looking at his world, his future. A lump started to form in his throat, and then his subconscious reminded him of the mission at hand. The icy calmness returned. He gently wrapped her petite body in his arms, shielding her from Ajeet's view, who was standing behind him now. He gently moved his hands over her back and front. No wires, no belts. She was clear.

Arthik unwrapped himself from Marge and stood up. He then turned around to face Ajeet. He was careful to keep himself between Ajeet and Marge.

"So now what, Arthik?" Ajeet said, and his lips touched a smile.

"I'm going to kill you," Arthik replied. His voice was matter-of-fact.

"I believe you," Ajeet said, pointing the gun at Arthik's midsection. "How?"

"I'm working on it," Arthik said. And now was the time to get Ajeet off his confident perch. "There's a cure for the bug."

"What? Cure for what?" Ajeet cocked his head.

"You know for what. It's on a flight from India right now," Arthik said. Ajeet was less than five feet away from him.

"You are bluffing. This is incurable—"

"I'm not, and it isn't. Colling is dead, and the wackos in Baltimore are contained and will be neutralized," Arthik said, in the same matter-of-fact tone.

Ajeet's eyes shifted. He looked around. The gun wavered. Arthik took a small step forward. It went unnoticed. A few more inches…

And then Arthik took a long step and flung himself on Ajeet. A shot rang out and a searing lance of pain went down Arthik's left arm. But that was of no consequence. The pent-up grief, frustration, and anger of the last few days overrode the pain by a mile. If Ajeet was going to blow himself up, he had to make sure Marge was safe.

Arthik knocked the gun out of Ajeet's right hand, and his arms wrapped around Ajeet in a vice-like grip. Kranken and Ricky came running up and separated the two.

"No bombs or belts on him," Ricky said, after patting down Ajeet.

Arthik picked up Ajeet's gun and pointed it at him.

"Hold on, Art," Kranken said.

"He has to die," Arthik said in a flat monotone. Arthik's shirt seeped red along his left arm.

"He will, but not today. We need him alive to get intel," Kranken said. "There might be more terrorists with this bug out there. And you need that arm looked at."

Arthik's head felt as if it was about to explode. The pain in the left arm was getting sharper.

"Killing him now will be the easy way out for him," Kranken took a step towards Arthik.

"Take the shot, my *Gabru Puttar*. Be a man. Avenge your family," Ajeet mumbled through broken teeth.

Arthik raised his arm and pointed the gun squarely at Ajeet's forehead.

"Don't do it, Art. We need to know what he knows," Kranken said, his tone firm.

Arthik closed his eyes for a long moment and let the gun clatter on the floor. In the next second, Arthik's heart and soul was seared by the events of the last few days. His family, Marge, Avtar and images of toddlers kissing neon-colored animals. He took a quick step forward, swinging his right fist and hit Ajeet as if he wanted to launch him into orbit. He hit him with all that was left in him. His anger, despair, grief and pain rolled onto his right fist as it made contact.

Ajeet fell back and lay still.

Arthik slumped on his knees and held his head in his hands. The pain in his left arm was real now. Kranken came up behind him.

"You did the right thing, Art," he said. "Let's get your arm looked at."

EPILOGUE

"THANKS FOR EVERYTHING," GORDO'S VOICE CRACK-led over the phone.

"Just don't ever call me again, Gordo," Kranken said as he got into his car.

"Even if the world is coming to an end?" A hint of a smile tinged Gordo's voice.

"Especially if the world is coming to an end," Kranken replied.

"Good luck, Joe. Enjoy your retirement. You deserve it." Gordo clicked the line dead.

Kranken drove to Loudoun Hospital Center. The hospital was a mile across from Loudoun County Fairgrounds. It had just been a week since the events at the circus, but it seemed a lifetime ago.

"Hi, John, how are you?" Kranken asked as he entered John Eter's hospital room.

"Here's the man himself. I'm doing really well," John said, his mouth splitting into a smile. "I believe you have met Rupani?" He pointed to the beautiful woman standing by the bed.

"I have had the pleasure," Kranken smiled back.

"Everything under control now, Joe?" Rupani asked.

"Yes, it is. All the bad guys are accounted for. How about the outbreak? I heard the US government appointed you co-chair of the task force," Kranken said.

"Yeah. We all were lucky to avoid a major catastrophe, though we still lost twenty-three people to the infection. The immunoglobulin serum is being produced at a war footing in Gaithersburg. The vaccine should be ready in a few months," Rupani said.

"And a lot of this is thanks to you, Joe," John said.

"Oh, I don't think so. It was a team effort," Kranken replied. "It was great working with you. Good luck."

Next stop for Joe was Arthik's apartment.

"Hi, Joe," Arthik said at the door.

"Hello, Art," Kranken said. "How's Marge?"

"C'mon in. She's here. Almost back to normal. Hey, Marge… Joe's here," Arthik called out to the bedroom.

"Hi Joe." Marge gave Joe a hug. "Thanks for everything."

"No need to thank me," Joe replied. "Thank the young man here," he said, pointing to Arthik.

"Where's Ajeet?" Arthik asked, his voice cold.

Joe paused for a moment.

"He is at a place where he can't hurt anyone," he replied.

"But where is he?" Arthik persisted.

Marge walked up to Arthik and held his hand.

"It's best if you don't know," Joe replied quietly. "He won't bother anyone ever again."

Arthik was silent.

"And one more thing, Gordo will get in touch with you. There's some reward money after they found a stash of cash at Ajeet's residence," Joe said.

"Reward? What—"

"I don't know the details. Gordo will explain that to you." Joe said, as he started to walk out.

"Wait…" Arthik said. "That's it? When do I see you again?"

Joe turned around and smiled.

"You don't," he replied. "Have a great life."